THE RETURN OF JEEVES

Available in Perennial Library
by P. G. Wodehouse

THE CAT-NAPPERS

HOW RIGHT YOU ARE, JEEVES

JEEVES AND THE FEUDAL SPIRIT

JEEVES AND THE TIE THAT BINDS

JEEVES IN THE MORNING

THE MATING SEASON

THE RETURN OF JEEVES

STIFF UPPER LIP, JEEVES

THANK YOU, JEEVES

THE WORLD OF JEEVES
(short stories)

P. G. WODEHOUSE

THE RETURN OF

PERENNIAL LIBRARY

Harper & Row, Publishers, New York
Grand Rapids, Philadelphia, St. Louis, San Francisco
London, Singapore, Sydney, Tokyo, Toronto

A hardcover edition of this book was published by Simon and Schuster, Inc. It is here reprinted by arrangement with the Estate of P. G. Wodehouse.

First PERENNIAL LIBRARY rack-size edition published 1985. PERENNIAL LIBRARY trade-size edition published 1990.

The Library of Congress has catalogued this title as follows:

Wodehouse, P. G. (Pelham Grenville), 1881–1975.
    The return of Jeeves.

    I. Title.
PR6045.O53R4   1985   823′.912   85–42606
ISBN 0–06–080768–7 (pbk.)

ISBN 0–06–096502–9 (pbk.)

90 91 92 93 94 MPC 10 9 8 7 6 5 4 3 2 1

THE RETURN OF JEEVES

∗ 1 ∗

THE waiter, who had slipped out to make a quick telephone call, came back into the coffee-room of the Goose and Gherkin wearing the starry-eyed look of a man who has just learned that he has backed a long-priced winner. He yearned to share his happiness with someone, and the only possible confidant was the woman at the table near the door, who was having a small gin and tonic and whiling away the time by reading a book of spiritualistic interest. He decided to tell her the good news.

"I don't know if you would care to know, madam," he said, in a voice that throbbed with emotion, "but Whistler's Mother won the Oaks."

The woman looked up, regarding him with large, dark, soulful eyes as if he had been something recently assembled from ectoplasm.

"The what?"

"The Oaks, madam."

"And what are the Oaks?"

It seemed incredible to the waiter that there should be anyone in England who could ask such a question, but he had already gathered that the lady was an American lady, and American ladies, he knew, are often ignorant of the fundamental facts of life. He had once met one who had wanted to know what a football pool was.

"It's an annual horse race, madam, reserved for fillies. By which I mean that it comes off once a year and the male sex isn't allowed to compete. It's run at Epsom Downs the day before the Derby, of which you have no doubt heard."

"Yes, I have heard of the Derby. It is your big race over here, is it not?"

"Yes, madam. What is sometimes termed a classic. The Oaks is run the day before it, though in previous years the day after. By which I mean," said the waiter, hoping he was not being too abstruse, "it used to be run the day following the Derby, but now they've changed it."

"And Whistler's Mother won this race you call the Oaks?"

7

"Yes, madam. By a couple of lengths. I was on five bob."

"I see. Well, that's fine, isn't it? Will you bring me another gin and tonic?"

"Certainly, madam. Whistler's Mother!" said the waiter, in a sort of ecstasy. "What a beauty!"

He went out. The woman resumed her reading. Quiet descended on the coffee-room.

In its general essentials the coffee-room at the Goose and Gherkin differed very little from the coffee-rooms of all the other inns that nestle by the wayside in England and keep the island race from dying of thirst. It had the usual dim religious light, the customary pictures of The Stag At Bay and The Huguenot's Farewell over the mantelpiece, the same cruets and bottles of sauce, and the traditional ozone-like smell of mixed pickles, gravy soup, boiled potatoes, waiters and old cheese.

What distinguished it on this June afternoon and gave it a certain something that the others had not got was the presence in it of the woman the waiter had been addressing. As a general rule, in the coffee-rooms of English wayside inns, all the eye is able to feast on is an occasional farmer eating fried eggs or a couple of commercial travellers telling each other improper stories, but the Goose and Gherkin had drawn this strikingly handsome hand across the sea, and she raised the tone of the place unbelievably.

The thing about her that immediately arrested the attention and drew the startled whistle to the lips was the aura of wealth which she exuded. It showed itself in her rings, her hat, her stockings, her shoes, her platinum fur cape and the Jacques Fath sports costume that clung lovingly to her undulating figure. Here, you would have said to yourself, beholding her, was a woman who had got the stuff in sackfuls and probably suffered agonies from coupon-clipper's thumb, a woman at the mention of whose name the blood-sucking leeches of the Internal Revenue Department were accustomed to raise their filthy hats with a reverent intake of the breath.

Nor would you have been in error. She was just as rich as she looked. Twice married and each time to a multi-millionaire, she was as nicely fixed financially as any woman could have wished.

Hers had been one of those Horatio Alger careers which are so encouraging to girls who hope to get on in the world, showing as they do that you never know what prizes Fate may be storing up for you around the corner. Born Rosalinda Banks, of the Chili-cothe, Ohio, Bankses, with no assets beyond a lovely face, a superb figure and a mild talent for *vers libre*, she had come to Greenwich Village to seek her fortune and had found it first crack out of the box. At a studio party in Macdougall Alley she had met and fascinated Clifton Bessemer, the Pulp Paper Magnate, and in almost no time at all had become his wife.

Widowed owing to Clifton Bessemer trying to drive his car one night through a truck instead of round it, and two years later meeting in Paris and marrying the millionaire sportsman and big game hunter, A. B. Spottsworth, she was almost immediately widowed again.

It was a confusion of ideas between him and one of the lions he was hunting in Kenya that had caused A. B. Spottsworth to make the obituary column. He thought the lion was dead, and the lion thought it wasn't. The result being that when he placed his foot on the animal's neck preparatory to being photographed by Captain Biggar, the White Hunter accompanying the expedition, a rather unpleasant brawl had ensued, and owing to Captain Biggar having to drop the camera and spend several vital moments looking about for his rifle, his bullet, though unerring, had come too late to be of practical assistance. There was nothing to be done but pick up the pieces and transfer the millionaire sportsman's vast fortune to his widow, adding it to the sixteen million or so which she had inherited from Clifton Bessemer.

Such, then, was Mrs. Spottsworth, a woman with a soul and about forty-two million dollars in the old oak chest. And, to clear up such minor points as may require elucidation, she was on her way to Rowcester Abbey, where she was to be the guest of the ninth Earl of Rowcester, and had stopped off at the Goose and Gherkin because she wanted to stretch her legs and air her Pekinese dog Pomona. She was reading a book of spiritualistic interest because she had recently become an enthusiastic devotee of psychical research. She was wearing a Jacques Fath sports costume because she liked Jacques Fath sports costumes. And she was drinking gin and tonic because it was one of those warm evenings when a gin and tonic just hits the spot.

The waiter returned with the elixir, and went on where he had left off.

"Thirty-three to one the price was, madam."

Mrs. Spottsworth raised her lustrous eyes.

"I beg your pardon?"

"That's what she started at."

"To whom do you refer?"

"This filly I was speaking of that's won the Oaks."

"Back to her, are we?" said Mrs. Spottsworth with a sigh. She had been reading about some interesting manifestations from the spirit world, and this earthy stuff jarred upon her.

The waiter sensed the lack of enthusiasm. It hurt him a little. On this day of days he would have preferred to have to do only with those in whose veins sporting blood ran.

"You're not fond of racing, madam?"

Mrs. Spottsworth considered.

"Not particularly. My first husband used to be crazy about it, but it always seemed to me so unspiritual. All that stuff about booting them home and goats and beetles and fast tracks and mudders and something he referred to as a boat race. Not at all the sort of thing to develop a person's higher self. I'd bet a grand now and then, just for the fun of it, but that's as far as I would go. It never touched the deeps in me."

"A grand, madam?"

"A thousand dollars."

"Coo!" said the waiter, awed. "That's what I'd call putting your shirt on. Though for me it'd be not only my shirt but my stockings and pantie-girdle as well. Lucky for the bookies you weren't at Epsom today, backing Whistler's Mother."

He moved off, and Mrs. Spottsworth resumed her book.

For perhaps ten minutes after that nothing of major importance happened in the coffee-room of the Goose and Gherkin except that the waiter killed a fly with his napkin and Mrs. Spottsworth finished her gin and tonic. Then the door was flung open by a powerful hand, and a tough, square, chunky, weather-beaten-looking man in the middle forties strode in. He had keen blue eyes, a very red face, a round head inclined to baldness and one of those small, bristly moustaches which abound in such profusion in the outposts of Empire. Indeed, these sprout in so widespread a way on the upper lips of those who bear the white man's burden that it is a tenable theory that the latter hold some sort of patent rights. One recalls the nostalgic words of the poet Kipling, when he sang "Put me somewhere east of Suez, where the best is like the worst, where there ain't no ten commandments and a man can raise a small bristly moustache."

It was probably this moustache that gave the newcomer the exotic look he had. It made him seem out of place in the coffee-room of an English inn. You felt, eyeing him, that his natural setting was Black Mike's bar in Pago-Pago, where he would be the life and soul of the party, though of course most of the time he would be out on safari, getting rough with such fauna as happened to come his way. Here, you would have said, was a man who many a time had looked his rhinoceros in the eye and made it wilt.

And again, just as when you were making that penetrating analysis of Mrs. Spottsworth, you would have been perfectly right. This bristly moustached he-man of the wilds was none other than the Captain Biggar whom we mentioned a moment ago in connection with the regrettable fracas which had culminated in A. B. Spottsworth going to reside with the morning stars, and any of the crowd out along Bubbling Well Road or in the Long Bar at Shanghai could have told you that "Bwana" Biggar had made more rhinoceri wilt than you could shake a stick at.

At the moment, he was thinking less of our dumb chums than of something cool in a tankard. The evening, as we have said, was warm, and he had driven many miles—from Epsom Downs, where he had started immediately after the conclusion of the race known as The Oaks, to this quiet inn in Southmoltonshire.

"Beer!" he thundered, and at the sound of his voice Mrs. Spottsworth dropped her book with a startled cry, her eyes leaping from the parent sockets.

And in the circumstances it was quite understandable that her eyes should have leaped, for her first impression had been that this was one of those interesting manifestations from the spirit world, of which she had been reading. Enough to make any woman's eyes leap.

The whole point about a hunter like Captain Biggar, if you face it squarely, is that he hunts. And, this being so, you expect him to stay put in and around his chosen hunting grounds. Meet him in Kenya or Malaya or Borneo or India, and you feel no surprise. "Hullo there, Captain Biggar," you say. "How's the spooring?" And he replies that the spooring is tophole. Everything perfectly in order.

But when you see him in the coffee-room of an English country inn, thousands of miles from his natural habitat, you may be excused for harbouring a momentary suspicion that this is not the man in the flesh but rather his wraith or phantasm looking in, as wraiths and phantasms will, to pass the time of day.

"Eek!" Mrs. Spottsworth exclaimed, visibly shaken. Since

interesting herself in psychical research, she had often wished to see a ghost, but one likes to pick one's time and place for that sort of thing. One does not want spectres muscling in when one is enjoying a refreshing gin and tonic.

To the Captain, owing to the dimness of the light in the Goose and Gherkin's coffee-room, Mrs. Spottsworth, until she spoke, had been simply a vague female figure having one for the road. On catching sight of her, he had automatically twirled his moustache, his invariable practice when he observed anything female in the offing, but he had in no sense drunk her in. Bending his gaze upon her now, he quivered all over like a nervous young hippopotamus finding itself face to face with its first White Hunter.

"Well, fry me in butter!" he ejaculated. He stood staring at her. "Mrs. Spottsworth! Well, simmer me in prune juice! Last person in the world I'd have dreamed of seeing. I thought you were in America."

Mrs. Spottsworth had recovered her poise.

"I flew over for a visit a week ago," she said.

"Oh, I see. That explains it. What made it seem odd, finding you here, was that I remember you told me you lived in California or one of those places."

"Yes, I have a home in Pasadena. In Carmel, too, and one in New York and another in Florida and another up in Maine."

"Making five in all?"

"Six. I was forgetting the one in Oregon."

"Six?" The Captain seemed thoughtful. "Oh, well," he said, "it's nice to have a roof over your head, of course."

"Yes. But one gets tired of places after a while. One yearns for something new. I'm thinking of buying this house I'm on my way to now, Rowcester Abbey. I met Lord Rowcester's sister in New York on her way back from Jamaica, and she said her brother might be willing to sell. But what are you doing in England, Captain? I couldn't believe my eyes at first."

"Oh, I thought I'd take a look at the old country, dear lady. Long time since I had a holiday, and you know the old proverb—all work and no play makes Jack a *peh-bah pom bahoo*. Amazing the way things have changed since I was here last. No idle rich, if you know what I mean. Everybody working. Everybody got a job of some kind."

"Yes, it's extraordinary, isn't it? Lord Rowcester's sister, Lady Carmoyle, tells me her husband, Sir Roderick Carmoyle, is a floorwalker at Harrige's. And he's a tenth Baronet or something."

"Amazing, what? Tubby Frobisher and the Subahdar won't believe me when I tell them."

"Who?"

"Couple of pals of mine out in Kuala Lumpur. They'll be astounded. But I like it," said the Captain stoutly. "It's the right spirit. The straight bat."

"I beg your pardon?"

"A cricket term, dear lady. At cricket you've got to play with a straight bat, or . . . or, let's face it, you don't play with a straight bat, if you see what I mean."

"I suppose so. But do sit down, won't you?"

"Thanks, if I may, but only for a minute. I'm chasing a foe of the human species."

In Captain Biggar's manner, as he sat down, a shrewd observer would have noted a trace of embarrassment, and might have attributed this to the fact that the last time he and Mrs. Spottsworth had seen each other he had been sorting out what was left of her husband with a view to shipping it to Nairobi. But it was not the memory of that awkward moment that was causing his diffidence. Its roots lay deeper than that.

He loved this woman. He had loved her from the very moment she had come into his life. How well he remembered that moment. The camp among the acacia trees. The boulder-strewn cliff. The boulder-filled stream. Old Simba the lion roaring in the distance, old Tembo the elephant doing this and that in the *bimbo* or tall grass, and A. B. Spottsworth driving up in the car with a vision in jodhpurs at his side. "My wife," A. B. Spottsworth had said, indicating the combination of Cleopatra and Helen of Troy by whom he was accompanied, and as he replied "Ah, the memsahib" and greeted her with a civil "*Krai yu ti ny ma pay*," it was as if a powerful electric shock had passed through Captain Biggar. This, he felt, was It.

Naturally, being a white man, he had not told his love, but it had burned steadily within him ever since, a strong, silent passion of such a calibre that sometimes, as he sat listening to the hyaenas and gazing at the snows of Kilimanjaro, it had brought him within an ace of writing poetry.

And here she was again, looking lovelier than ever. It seemed to Captain Biggar that somebody in the vicinity was beating a bass drum. But it was only the thumping of his heart.

His last words had left Mrs. Spottsworth fogged.

"Chasing a foe of the human species?" she queried.

"A blighter of a bookie. A cad of the lowest order with a soul as black as his finger-nails. I've been after him for hours. And I'd have caught him," said the captain, moodily sipping beer, "if something hadn't gone wrong with my bally car. They're fixing it now at that garage down the road."

"But why were you chasing this bookmaker?" asked Mrs. Spottsworth. It seemed to her a frivolous way for a strong man to be passing his time.

Captain Biggar's face darkened. Her question had touched an exposed nerve.

"The low hound did the dirty on me. Seemed straight enough, too. Chap with a walrus moustache and a patch over his left eye. Honest Patch Perkins, he called himself. 'Back your fancy and fear nothing, my noble sportsman,' he said. 'If you don't specu-late, you can't accumulate,' he said. 'Walk up, walk up. Roll, bowl or pitch. Ladies half-way and no bad nuts returned,' he said. So I put my double on with him."

"Your double?"

"A double, dear lady, is when you back a horse in one race and if it wins, put the proceeds on another horse in another race."

"Oh, what we call a parlay in America."

"Well, you can readily see that if both bounders pull it off, you pouch a princely sum. I've got in with a pretty knowledgeable crowd since I came to London, and they recommended as a good double for today Lucy Glitters and Whistler's Mother."

The name struck a chord.

"The waiter was telling me that Whistler's Mother won."

"So did Lucy Glitters in the previous race. I had a fiver on her at a hundred to six and all to come on Whistler's Mother for the Oaks. She ambled past the winning post at——"

"Thirty-three to one, the waiter was saying. My goodness! You certainly cleaned up, didn't you!"

Captain Biggar finished his beer. If it is possible to drink beer like an overwrought soul, he did so.

"I certainly ought to have cleaned up," he said, with a heavy frown. "There was the colossal sum of three thousand pounds two shillings and sixpence owing to me, plus my original fiver which I had handed to the fellow's clerk, a chap in a check suit and another walrus moustache. And what happened? This inky-hearted bookie

welshed on me. He legged it in his car with me after him. I've been
pursuing him, winding and twisting through the country roads,
for what seems an eternity. And just as I was on the point of
grappling with him, my car broke down. But I'll have the scoundrel! I'll catch the louse! And when I do, I propose to scoop out
his insides with my bare hands and twist his head off and make
him swallow it. After which——"

Captain Biggar broke off. It had suddenly come to him that he
was monopolizing the conversation. After all, of what interest
could these daydreams of his be to this woman?

"But let's not talk about me any more," he said. "Dull subject.
How have you been all these years, dear lady? Pretty fit, I hope?
You look right in the pink. And how's your husband? Oh, sorry!"

"Not at all. You mean, have I married again? No, I have not
married again, though Clifton and Alexis keep advising me to.
They are sweet about it. So broad-minded and considerate."

"Clifton? Alexis?"

"Mr. Bessemer and Mr. Spottsworth, my two previous husbands. I get them on the ouija board from time to time. I suppose," said Mrs. Spottsworth, laughing a little self-consciously,
"you think it's odd of me to believe in things like the ouija
board?"

"Odd?"

"So many of my friends in America call all that sort of thing
poppycock."

Captain Biggar snorted militantly.

"I'd like to be there to talk to them! I'd astonish their weak
intellects. No, dear lady, I've seen too many strange things in my
time, living as I have done in the shadow-lands of mystery, to
think anything odd. I have seen barefooted pilgrims treading the
path of Ahura-Mazda over burning coals. I've seen ropes tossed
in the air and small boys shinning up them in swarms. I've met
fakirs who slept on beds of spikes."

"Really?"

"I assure you. And think of it, insomnia practically unknown.
So you don't catch me laughing at people because they believe in
ouija boards."

Mrs. Spottsworth gazed at him tenderly. She was thinking how
sympathetic and understanding he was.

"I am intensely interested in psychical research. I am proud to
be one of the little band of devoted seekers who are striving to

pierce the veil. I am hoping to be vouchsafed some enthralling spiritual manifestation at this Rowcester Abbey where I'm going. It is one of the oldest houses in England, they tell me."

"Then you ought to flush a spectre or two," agreed Captain Biggar. "They collect in gangs in these old English country houses. How about another gin and tonic?"

"No, I must be getting along. Pomona's in the car, and she hates being left alone."

"You couldn't stay and have one more quick one?"

"I fear not. I must be on my way. I can't tell you how delightful it has been, meeting you again, Captain."

"Just made my day, meeting you, dear lady," said Captain Biggar, speaking hoarsely, for he was deeply moved. They were out in the open now, and he was able to get a clearer view of her as she stood beside her car bathed in the sunset glow. How lovely she was, he felt, how wonderful, how . . . Come, come, Biggar, he said to himself gruffly, this won't do, old chap. Play the game, Biggar, play the game, old boy!

"Won't you come and see me when I get back to London, Captain? I shall be at the Savoy."

"Charmed, dear lady, charmed," said Captain Biggar. But he did not mean it.

For what would be the use? What would it profit him to renew their acquaintance? Just twisting the knife in the wound, that's what he would be doing. Better, far better, to bite the bullet and wash the whole thing out here and now. A humble hunter with scarcely a bob to his name couldn't go mixing with wealthy widows. It was the kind of thing he had so often heard Tubby Frobisher and the Subahdar denouncing in the old Anglo-Malay Club at Kuala Lumpur. "Chap's nothing but a bally fortune-hunter, old boy," they would say, discussing over the gin *pahits* some acquaintance who had made a rich marriage. "Simply a blighted gigolo, old boy, nothing more. Can't do that sort of thing, old chap, what? Not cricket, old boy."

And they were right. It couldn't be done. Damn it all, a feller had his code. "*Meh nee pan kong bahn rotfai*" about summed it up.

Stiffening his upper lip, Captain Biggar went down the road to see how his car was getting on.

Rowcester Abbey—pronounced Roaster—was about ten miles from the Goose and Gherkin. It stood—such portions of it as had not fallen down—just beyond Southmolton in the midst of smiling country. Though if you had asked William Egerton Bamfylde Ossingham Belfry, ninth Earl of Rowcester, its proprietor, what the English countryside had to smile about these days, he would have been unable to tell you. Its architecture was thirteenth century, fifteenth century and Tudor, its dilapidation twentieth century post-World War Two.

To reach the Abbey you turned off the main road and approached by a mile-long drive thickly incrusted with picturesque weeds and made your way up stone steps, chipped in spots, to a massive front door which badly needed a lick of paint. And this was what Bill Rowcester's sister Monica and her husband, Sir Roderick ("Rory") Carmoyle, had done at just about the hour when Mrs. Spottsworth and Captain Biggar were starting to pick up the threads at their recent reunion.

Monica, usually addressed as Moke, was small and vivacious, her husband large and stolid. There was something about his aspect and deportment that suggested a more than ordinarily placid buffalo chewing a cud and taking in its surroundings very slowly and methodically, refusing to be hurried. It was thus that, as they stood on the front steps, he took in Rowcester Abbey.

"Moke," he said at length, having completed his scrutiny, "I'll tell you something which you may or may not see fit to release to the Press. This bally place looks mouldier every time I see it."

Monica was quick to defend her childhood home.

"It might be a lot worse."

Rory considered this, chewing his cud for a while in silence.

"How?" he asked.

"I know it needs doing up, but where's the money to come from? Poor old Bill can't afford to run a castle on a cottage income."

"Why doesn't he get a job like the rest of us?"

"You needn't stick on side just because you're in trade, you old counterjumper."

"Everybody's doing it, I mean to say. Nowadays the House of Lords is practically empty except on evenings and bank holidays."

"We Rowcesters aren't easy to place. The Rowcester men have all been lilies of the field. Why, Uncle George didn't even put on his own boots."

"Whose boots did he put on?" asked Rory, interested.

"Ah, that's what we'd all like to know. Of course, Bill's big mistake was letting that American woman get away from him."

"What American woman would that be?"

"It was just after you and I got married. A Mrs. Bessemer. A widow. He met her in Cannes one summer. Fabulously rich and, according to Bill, unimaginably beautiful. It seemed promising for a time, but it didn't come to anything. I suppose someone cut him out. Of course, he was plain Mr. Belfry then, not my lord Rowcester, which may have made a difference."

Rory shook his head.

"It wouldn't be that. I was plain Mr. Carmoyle when I met you and look at the way I snaffled you in the teeth of the pick of the County."

"But then think what you were like in those days. A flick of the finger, a broken heart. And you're not so bad now, either," added Monica fondly. "Something of the old magic remains."

"True," said Rory placidly. "In a dim light I still cast a spell. But the trouble with Bill was, I imagine, that he lacked *drive* . . . the sort of drive you see so much of at Harrige's. The will to win, I suppose you might call it. Napoleon had it. I have it, Bill hasn't. Oh, well, there it is," said Rory philosophically. He resumed his study of Rowcester Abbey. "You know what this house wants?" he proceeded. "An atom bomb, dropped carefully on the roof of the main banqueting hall."

"It would help, wouldn't it?"

"It would be the making of the old place. Put it right in no time. Still, atom bombs cost money, so I suppose that's out of the question. What you ought to do is use your influence with Bill to persuade him to buy a lot of paraffin and some shavings and save the morning papers and lay in plenty of matches and wait till some moonless night and give the joint the works. He'd feel a different man, once the old ruin was nicely ablaze."

Monica looked mysterious.

"I can do better than that."

Rory shook his head.

"No. Arson. It's the only way. You can't beat good old arson. Those fellows down in the east end go in for it a lot. They touch a match to the shop, and it's like a week at the seaside to them."

"What would you say if I told you I was hoping to sell the house?"

Rory stared, amazed. He had a high opinion of his wife's resourcefulness, but he felt that she was attempting the impossible.

"Sell it? I don't believe you could give it away. I happen to know Bill offered it for a song to one of these charitable societies as a Home for Reclaimed Juvenile Delinquents, and they simply sneered at him. Probably thought it would give the Delinquents rheumatism. Very damp house, this."

"It is a bit moist."

"Water comes through the walls in heaping handfuls. I suppose because it's so close to the river. I remember saying to Bill once, 'Bill,' I said, 'I'll tell you something about your home surroundings. In the summer the river is at the bottom of your garden, and in the winter your garden is at the bottom of the river.' Amused the old boy quite a bit. He thought it clever."

Monica regarded her husband with that cold, wifely eye which married men learn to dread.

"Very clever," she said frostily. "Extremely droll. And I suppose the first thing you'll do is make a crack like that to Mrs. Spottsworth."

"Eh?" It stole slowly into Rory's mind that a name had been mentioned that was strange to him. "Who's Mrs. Spottsworth?"

"The woman I'm hoping to sell the house to. American. Very rich. I met her when I was passing through New York on my way home. She owns dozens of houses in America, but she's got a craving to have something old and picturesque in England."

"Romantic, eh?"

"Dripping with romance. Well, when she told me that—we were sitting next to each other at a women's lunch—I immediately thought of Bill and the Abbey, of course, and started giving her a sales talk. She seemed interested. After all, the Abbey is chock full of historical associations."

"And mice."

"She was flying to England next day, so I told her when I would be arriving and we arranged that she was to come here and have a look at the place. She should be turning up at any moment."

"Does Bill know she's coming?"

"No. I ought to have sent him a cable, but I forgot. Still, what does it matter? He'll be only too delighted. The important thing is to keep you from putting her off with your mordant witticisms. 'I often say in my amusing way, Mrs. Spottsworth, that whereas in the summer months the river is at the bottom of the garden, in the winter months—ha, ha—the garden—this is going to slay you—is at the bottom of the river, ho, ho, ho.' That would just clinch the sale."

"Now would I be likely to drop a brick of that sort, old egg?"

"Extremely likely, old crumpet. The trouble with you is that, though a king among men, you have no tact."

Rory smiled. The charge tickled him.

"No tact? The boys at Harrige's would laugh if they heard that."

"Do remember that it's vital to put this deal through."

"I'll bear it in mind. I'm all for giving poor old Bill a leg-up. It's a damn shame," said Rory, who often thought rather deeply on these subjects. "Bill starts at the bottom of the ladder as a mere heir to an Earldom, and by pluck and perseverance works his way up till he becomes the Earl himself. And no sooner has he settled the coronet on his head and said to himself 'Now to whoop it up!' than they pull a social revolution out of their hats like a rabbit and snitch practically every penny he's got. Ah, well!" said Rory with a sigh. "I say," he went on, changing the subject, "have you noticed, Moke, old girl, that throughout this little chat of ours—which I for one have thoroughly enjoyed—I have been pressing the bell at frequent intervals and not a damn thing has happened? What is this joint, the palace of the sleeping beauty? Or do you think the entire strength of the company has been wiped out by some plague or pestilence?"

"Good heavens!" said Monica, "bells at Rowcester Abbey don't ring. I don't suppose they've worked since Edward the Seventh's days. If Uncle George wished to summon the domestic staff, he just shoved his head back and howled like a prairie wolf."

"That would have been, I take it, when he wanted somebody else's boots to put on?"

"You just open the door and walk in. Which is what I am about to do now. You bring the bags in from the car."

"Depositing them where?"

"In the hall for the moment," said Monica. "You can take them upstairs later."

She went in, and made her way to that familiar haunt, the living-room off the hall where in her childhood days most of the life of Rowcester Abbey had centred. Like other English houses of its size, the Abbey had a number of vast state apartments which were never used, a library which was used occasionally, and this living-room, the popular meeting-place. It was here that in earlier days she had sat and read the *Girl's Own Paper* and, until the veto had been placed on her activities by her Uncle George, whose sense of smell was acute, had kept white rabbits. A big, comfortable, shabby room with French windows opening into the garden, at the bottom of which—in the summer months—the river ran.

As she stood looking about her, sniffing the old familiar smell of tobacco and leather and experiencing, as always, a nostalgic thrill and a vague wish that it were possible to put the clock back, there came through the French window a girl in overalls, who, having stared for a moment in astonishment, uttered a delighted squeal.

"Moke . . . *darling!*"

Monica turned.

"Jill, my angel!"

They flung themselves into each other's arms.

★ 3 ★

Jill Wyvern was young, very pretty, slightly freckled and obviously extremely practical and competent. She wore her overalls as if they had been a uniform. Like Monica, she was small, and an admirer of hers, from Bloomsbury, had once compared her, in an unpublished poem, to a Tanagra statuette. It was not a very apt comparison, for Tanagra statuettes, whatever their merits, are on the static side and Jill was intensely alert and alive. She moved with a springy step and in her time had been a flashy outside-right on the hockey field.

"My precious Moke," she said. "Is it really you? I thought you were in Jamaica."

"I got back this morning. I picked up Rory in London, and we motored down here. Rory's outside, looking after the bags."

"How brown you are!"

"That's Montego Bay. I worked on this sunburn for three months."

"It suits you. But Bill didn't say anything about expecting you. Aren't you appearing rather suddenly?"

"Yes, I cut my travels short rather suddenly. My allowance met those New York prices and gave up the ghost with a low moan. Ah, here's the merchant prince."

Rory came in, mopping his forehead.

"What have you got in those bags of yours, old girl? Lead?" He saw Jill, and stopped, gazing at her with wrinkled brow. "Oh, hullo," he said uncertainly.

"You remember Jill Wyvern, Rory."

"Of course, yes. Jill Wyvern, to be sure. As you so sensibly observe, Jill Wyvern. You been telling her about your sunburn?"

"She noticed it for herself."

"It does catch the eye. She says she's that colour all over," said Rory confidentially to Jill. "Might raise a question or two from an old-fashioned husband, what? Still, I suppose it all makes for variety. So you're Jill Wyvern, are you? How you've grown!"

"Since when?"

"Since . . . since you started growing."

"You haven't a notion who I am, have you?"

22

"I wouldn't say *that* . . ."

"I'll help you out. I was at your wedding."

"You don't look old enough."

"I was fifteen. They gave me the job of keeping the dogs from jumping on the guests. It was pouring, you may remember, and they all had muddy paws."

"Good God! Now I have you placed. So *you* were that little squirt. I noticed you bobbing about and thought what a frightful young excrescence you looked."

"My husband is noted for the polish of his manners," said Monica. "He is often called the modern Chesterfield."

"What I was about to add," said Rory with dignity, "was that she's come on a lot since those days, showing that we should never despair. But didn't we meet again some time?"

"Yes, a year or two later when you stayed here one summer. I was just coming out then, and I expect I looked more of an excrescence than ever."

Monica sighed.

"Coming out! The dear old getting-ready-for-market stage! How it takes one back. Off with the glasses and the teeth-braces."

"On with things that push you in or push you out, whichever you needed."

This was Rory's contribution, and Monica looked at him austerely.

"What do you know about it?"

"Oh, I get around in our Ladies' Foundation department," said Rory.

Jill laughed.

"What I remember best are those agonized family conferences about my hockey-player's hands. I used to walk about for hours holding them in the air."

"And how did you make out? Has it paid off yet?"

"Paid off?"

Monica lowered her voice confidentially.

"A man, dear. Did you catch anything worth while?"

"I think he's worth while. As a matter of fact, you don't know it, but you're moving in rather exalted circles. She whom you see before you is none other than the future Countess of Rowcester."

Monica screamed excitedly.

"You don't mean you and Bill are engaged?"

"That's right."

"Since when?"

"Some weeks ago."

"I'm delighted. I wouldn't have thought Bill had so much sense."

"No," agreed Rory in his tactful way. "One raises the eyebrows in astonishment. Bill, as I remember it, was always more of a lad for the buxom, voluptuous type. Many a passionate romance have I seen him through with females who looked like a cross between pantomime Fairy Queens and all-in wrestlers. There was a girl in the Hippodrome chorus——"

He broke off these reminiscences, so fraught with interest to a fiancée, in order to say "Ouch!" Monica had kicked him shrewdly on the ankle.

"Tell me, darling," said Monica. "How did it happen? Suddenly?"

"Quite suddenly. He was helping me give a cow a bolus——"

Rory blinked. "A——?"

"Bolus. Medicine. You give it to cows. And before I knew what was happening, he had grabbed my hand and was saying, 'I say, arising from this, will you marry me?' "

"How frightfully eloquent. When Rory proposed to me, all he said was 'Eh, what?' "

"And it took me three weeks to work up to that," said Rory. His forehead had become wrinkled again. It was plain that he was puzzling over something. "This bolus of which you were speaking. I don't quite follow. You were giving it to a cow, you say?"

"A sick cow."

"Oh, a sick cow? Well, here's the point that's perplexing me. Here's the thing that seems to me to need straightening out. *Why* were you giving boluses to sick cows?"

"It's my job. I'm the local vet."

"What! You don't by any chance mean a veterinary surgeon?"

"That's right. Fully licensed. We're all workers nowadays."

Rory nodded sagely.

"Profoundly true," he said. "I'm a son of toil myself."

"Rory's at Harrige's," said Monica.

"Really?"

"Floorwalker in the Hosepipe, Lawn Mower and Bird Bath department," said Rory. "But that is merely temporary. There's a strong rumour going the rounds that hints at promotion to the Glass, Fancy Goods and Chinaware. And from there to the Ladies' Underclothing is but a step."

"My hero!" Monica kissed him lovingly. "I'll bet they'll all be green with jealousy."

Rory was shocked at the suggestion.

"Good God, no! They'll rush to shake me by the hand and slap me on the back. Our *esprit de corps* is wonderful. It's one for all and all for one in Harrige's."

Monica turned back to Jill.

"And doesn't your father mind you running about the country giving boluses to cows? Jill's father," she explained to Rory, "is Chief Constable of the county."

"And very nice, too," said Rory.

"I should have thought he would have objected."

"Oh, no. We're all working at something. Except my brother Eustace. He won a Littlewood's pool last winter and he's gone frightfully upper class. Very high hat with the rest of the family. Moves on a different plane."

"Damn snob," said Rory warmly. "I hate class distinctions."

He was about to speak further, for the subject was one on which he held strong opinions, but at this moment the telephone bell rang, and he looked round, startled.

"For heaven's sake! Don't tell me the old boy has paid his telephone bill!" he cried, astounded.

Monica took up the receiver.

"Hullo? . . . Yes, this is Rowcester Abbey . . . No, Lord Rowcester is not in at the moment. This is his sister, Lady Carmoyle. The number of his car? It's news to me that he's *got* a car." She turned to Jill. "You don't know the number of Bill's car, do you?"

"No. Why are they asking?"

"Why are you asking?" said Monica into the telephone. She waited a moment, then hung up. "He's rung off."

"Who was it?"

"He didn't say. Just a voice from the void."

"You don't think Bill's had an accident?"

"Good heavens, no," said Rory. "He's much too good a driver. Probably he had to stop somewhere to buy some juice, and they need his number for their books. But it's always disturbing when people don't give their names on the telephone. There was a fellow in ours—second in command in the Jams, Sauces and Potted Meats—who was rung up one night by a Mystery Voice that wouldn't give its name, and to cut a long story short——"

Monica did so.

"Save it up for after dinner, my king of raconteurs," she said. "If there is any dinner," she added doubtfully.

"Oh, there'll be dinner all right," said Jill, "and you'll probably find it'll melt in the mouth. Bill's got a very good cook."

Monica stared.

"A cook? These days? I don't believe it. You'll be telling me next he's got a housemaid."

"He has. Name of Ellen."

"Pull yourself together, child. You're talking wildly. Nobody has a housemaid."

"Bill has. And a gardener. And a butler. A wonderful butler called Jeeves. And he's thinking of getting a boy to clean the knives and boots."

"Good heavens! It sounds like the home life of the Aga Khan." Monica frowned thoughtfully. "Jeeves?" she said. "Why does that name seem to ring a bell?"

Rory supplied illumination.

"Bertie Wooster. He has a man named Jeeves. This is probably a brother or an aunt or something."

"No," said Jill. "It's the same man. Bill has him on lend-lease."

"But how on earth does Bertie get on without him?"

"I believe Mr. Wooster's away somewhere. Anyhow, Jeeves appeared one day and said he was willing to take office, so Bill grabbed him, of course. He's an absolute treasure. Bill says he's an 'old soul,' whatever that means."

Monica was still bewildered.

"But how about the financial end? Does he pay this entourage, or just give them a pleasant smile now and then?"

"Of course he pays them. Lavishly. He flings them purses of gold every Saturday morning."

"Where does the money come from?"

"He earns it."

"Don't be silly. Bill hasn't earned a penny since he was paid twopence a time for taking his castor oil. How could he possibly earn it?"

"He's doing some sort of work for the Agricultural Board."

"You don't make a fortune out of that."

"Bill seems to. I suppose he's so frightfully good at his job that they pay him more than the others. I don't know what he does, actually. He just goes off in his car. Some kind of inspection, I suppose it is. Checking up on all those questionnaires. He's not very good at figures, so he always takes Jeeves with him."

"Well, that's wonderful," said Monica. "I was afraid he might have started backing horses again. It used to worry me so much in the old days, the way he would dash from race-course to race-course in a grey topper that he carried sandwiches in."

"Oh, no, it couldn't be anything like that. He promised me faithfully he would never bet on a horse again."

"Very sensible," said Rory. "I don't mind a flutter from time to time, of course. At Harrige's we always run a Sweep on big events, five-bob chances. The brass hats frown on anything larger."

Jill moved to the French window.

"Well, I mustn't stand here talking," she said. "I've got work to do. I came to attend to Bill's Irish terrier. It's sick of a fever."

"Give it a bolus."

"I'm giving it some new American ointment. It's got mange. See you later."

Jill went off on her errand of mercy, and Rory turned to Monica. His customary stolidity had vanished. He was keen and alert, like Sherlock Holmes on the trail.

"Moke!"

"Hullo?"

"What do you make of it, old girl?"

"Make of what?"

"This sudden affluence of Bill's. There's something fishy going on here. If it had just been a matter of a simple butler, one could have understood it. A broker's man in disguise, one would have said. But how about the housemaid and the cook and the car and, by Jove, the fact that he's paid his telephone bill."

"I see what you mean. It's odd."

"It's more than odd. Consider the facts. The last time I was at Rowcester Abbey, Bill was in the normal state of destitution of the upper-class Englishman of today, stealing the cat's milk and nosing about in the gutters for cigar-ends. I come here now, and what do I find? Butlers in every nook and cranny, housemaids as far as the eye can reach, cooks jostling each other in the kitchen, Irish terriers everywhere, and a lot of sensational talk going on about boys to clean the knives and boots. It's . . . what's the word?"

"I don't know."

"Yes, you do. Begins with 'in'."

"Influential? Inspirational? Infra red?"

"Inexplicable. That's what it is. The whole thing is utterly inexplicable. One dismisses all that stuff about jobs with the Agricultural Board as pure eyewash. You don't cut a stupendous dash like this on a salary from the Agricultural Board." Rory paused, and ruminated for a moment. "I wonder if the old boy's been launching out as a gentleman burglar."

"Don't be an idiot."

"Well, fellows do, you know. Raffles, if you remember. He was one, and made a dashed good thing out of it. Or could it be that he's blackmailing somebody?"

"Oh, Rory."

"Very profitable, I believe. You look around for some wealthy bimbo and nose out his guilty secrets, then you send him a letter saying that you know all and tell him to leave ten thousand quid in small notes under the second milestone on the London road. When you've spent that, you tap him for another ten. It all mounts up over a period of time, and would explain these butlers, housemaids and what not very neatly."

"If you would talk less drivel and take more bags upstairs, the world would be a better place."

Rory thought it over and got her meaning.

"You want me to take the bags upstairs?"

"I do."

"Right ho. The Harrige motto is Service."

The telephone rang again. Rory went to it.

"Hullo?" He started violently. "The *who*? Good God! All right. He's out now, but I'll tell him when I see him." He hung up. There was a grave look on his face. "Moke," he said, "perhaps you'll believe me another time and not scoff and mock when I advance my theories. That was the police."

"The police?"

"They want to talk to Bill."

"What about?"

"They didn't say. Well, dash it, they wouldn't, would they? Official Secrets Acts and all that sort of thing. But they're closing in on him, old girl, closing in on him."

"Probably all they want is to get him to present the prizes at the police sports or something."

"I doubt it," said Rory. "Still, hold that thought if it makes you happier. Take the bags upstairs, you were saying? I'll do it instanter. Come along and encourage me with word and gesture."

FOR some moments after they had gone the peace of the summer evening was broken only by the dull, bumping sound of a husband carrying suit-cases upstairs. This died away, and once more a drowsy stillness stole over Rowcester Abbey. Then, faintly at first but growing louder, there came from the distance the chugging of a car. It stopped, and there entered through the French window a young man. He tottered in, breathing heavily like a hart that pants for cooling streams when heated in the chase, and having produced his cigarette-case lit a cigarette in an over-wrought way, as if he had much on his mind.

Or what one may loosely call his mind. William, ninth Earl of Rowcester, though intensely amiable and beloved by all who knew him, was far from being a mental giant. From his earliest years his intimates had been aware that, while his heart was unquestionably in the right place, there was a marked shortage of the little grey cells, and it was generally agreed that whoever won the next Nobel prize, it would not be Bill Rowcester. At the Drones Club, of which he had been a member since leaving school, it was estimated that in the matter of intellect he ranked somewhere in between Freddie Widgeon and Pongo Twistleton, which is pretty low down on the list. There were some, indeed, who held his I.Q. to be inferior to that of Barmy Fotheringay-Phipps.

Against this must be set the fact that, like all his family, he was extremely good-looking, though those who considered him so might have revised their views, had they seen him now. For in addition to wearing a very loud check coat with bulging, volu-minous pockets and a crimson tie with blue horseshoes on it which smote the beholder like a blow, he had a large black patch over his left eye and on his upper lip a ginger moustache of the outsize or soupstrainer type. In the clean-shaven world in which we live today it is not often that one sees a moustache of this almost tropical luxuriance, and it is not often, it may be added, that one wants to.

A black patch and a ginger moustache are grave defects, but that the ninth Earl was not wholly dead to a sense of shame was shown by the convulsive start, like the leap of an adagio dancer, which he gave a moment later when, wandering about the room, he suddenly caught sight of himself in an old-world mirror that hung on the wall.

"Good Lord!" he exclaimed, recoiling.

With nervous fingers he removed the patch, thrust it into his pocket, tore the fungoid growth from his lip and struggled out of the check coat. This done, he went to the window, leaned out and called in a low, conspiratorial voice.

"Jeeves!"

There was no answer.

"Hi, Jeeves, where are you?"

Again silence.

Bill gave a whistle, then another. He was still whistling, his body half-way through the French window, when the door behind him opened, revealing a stately form.

The man who entered—or perhaps one should say shimmered into—the room was tall and dark and impressive. He might have been one of the better-class ambassadors or the youngish High Priest of some refined and dignified religion. His eyes gleamed with the light of intelligence, and his finely chiselled face expressed a feudal desire to be of service. His whole air was that of a gentleman's gentleman who, having developed his brain over a course of years by means of a steady fish diet, is eager to place that brain at the disposal of the young master. He was carrying over one arm a coat of sedate colour and a tie of conservative pattern.

"You whistled, m'lord?" he said.

Bill spun round.

"How the dickens did you get over there, Jeeves?"

"I ran the car into the garage, m'lord, and then made my way to the servants' quarters. Your coat, m'lord."

"Oh, thanks. I see you've changed."

"I deemed it advisable, m'lord. The gentleman was not far behind us as we rounded into the straight and may at any moment be calling. Were he to encounter on the threshold a butler in a check suit and a false moustache, it is possible that his suspicions might be aroused. I am glad to see that your lordship has removed that somewhat distinctive tie. Excellent for creating atmosphere on the racecourse, it is scarcely vogue in private life."

Bill eyed the repellent object with a shudder.

"I've always hated that beastly thing, Jeeves. All those foul horseshoes. Shove it away somewhere. And the coat."

"Very good, m'lord. This coffer should prove adequate as a temporary receptacle." Jeeves took the coat and tie, and crossed the room to where a fine old oak dower chest stood, an heirloom long in the Rowcester family. "Yes," he said, " 'Tis not so deep as a well nor so wide as a church door, but 'tis enough, 'twill serve."

He folded the distressing objects carefully, placed them inside and closed the lid. And even this simple act he performed with a quiet dignity which would have impressed any spectator less agitated than Bill Rowcester. It was like seeing the plenipotentiary of a great nation lay a wreath on the tomb of a deceased monarch.

But Bill, as we say, was agitated. He was brooding over an earlier remark that had fallen from this great man's lips.

"What do you mean, the gentleman may at any moment be calling?" he asked. The thought of receiving a visit from that red-faced man with the loud voice who had bellowed abuse at him all the way from Epsom Downs to Southmoltonshire was not an unmixedly agreeable one.

"It is possible that he observed and memorized the number of our car, m'lord. He was in a position to study our licence plate for some considerable time, your lordship will recollect."

Bill sank limply into a chair and brushed a bead of perspiration from his forehead. This contingency, as Jeeves would have called it, had not occurred to him. Placed before him now, it made him feel filleted.

"Oh, golly, I never thought of that. Then he would get the owner's name and come racing along here, wouldn't he?"

"So one would be disposed to imagine, m'lord."

"Hell's bells, Jeeves!"

"Yes, m'lord."

Bill applied the handkerchief to his forehead again.

"What do I do if he does?"

"I would advise your lordship to assume a nonchalant air and disclaim all knowledge of the matter."

"With a light laugh, you mean?"

"Precisely, m'lord."

Bill tried a light laugh. "How did that sound, Jeeves?"

"Barely adequate, m'lord."

"More like a death rattle?"

"Yes, m'lord."

"I shall need a few rehearsals."

"Several, m'lord. It will be essential to carry conviction."

Bill kicked petulantly at a footstool.

"How do you expect me to carry conviction, feeling the way I do?"

"I can readily appreciate that your lordship is disturbed."

"I'm all of a twitter. Have you ever seen a jelly hit by a cyclone?"

"No, m'lord, I have never been present on such an occasion."

"It quivers. So do I."

"After such an ordeal your lordship would be unstrung."

"Ordeal is the right word, Jeeves. Apart from the frightful peril one is in, it was so dashed ignominious having to leg it like that."

"I should hardly describe our recent activities as legging it, m'lord. 'Strategic retreat' is more the *mot juste*. This is a recognized military manœuvre, practised by all the greatest tacticians when the occasion seemed to call for such a move. I have no doubt that General Eisenhower has had recourse to it from time to time."

"But I don't suppose he had a fermenting punter after him, shouting 'Welsher!' at the top of his voice."

"Possibly not, m'lord."

Bill brooded. "It was that word 'Welsher' that hurt, Jeeves."

"I can readily imagine it, m'lord. Objected to as irrelevant, incompetent and immaterial, as I believe the legal expression is. As your lordship several times asseverated during our precarious homeward journey, you have every intention of paying the gentleman."

"Of course I have. No argument about that. Naturally I intend to brass up to the last penny. It's a case of . . . what, Jeeves?"

"*Noblesse oblige*, m'lord."

"Exactly. The honour of the Rowcesters is at stake. But I must have time, dash it, to raise three thousand pounds two and six."

"Three thousand and five pounds two and six, m'lord. Your lordship is forgetting the gentleman's original five-pound note."

"So I am. You trousered it and came away with it in your pocket."

"Precisely, m'lord. Thus bringing the sum total of your obligations to this Captain Biggar——"

"Was that his name?"

"Yes, m'lord. Captain C. G. Brabazon-Biggar, United Rovers Club, Northumberland Avenue, London W.C.2. In my capacity as your lordship's clerk I wrote the name and address on the ticket which he now has in his possession. The note which he handed to me and which I duly accepted as your lordship's official representative raises your commitments to three thousand and five pounds two shillings and sixpence."

"Oh, gosh!"

"Yes, m'lord. It is not an insignificant sum. Many a poor man would be glad of three thousand and five pounds two shillings and sixpence."

Bill winced. "I would be grateful, Jeeves, if you could see your way not to keep on intoning those words."

"Very good, m'lord."

"They are splashed on my soul in glorious technicolor."

"Quite so, m'lord."

"Who was it who said that when he or she was dead, the word something would be found carved on his or her heart?"

"Queen Mary, m'lord, the predecessor of the great Queen Elizabeth. The word was 'Calais', and the observation was intended to convey her chagrin at the loss of that town."

"Well, when I die, which will be very shortly if I go on feeling as I do now, just cut me open, Jeeves——"

"Certainly, m'lord."

"——and I'll bet you a couple of bob you'll find carved on my heart the words 'Three thousand and five pounds two and six'."

Bill rose and paced the room with fevered steps.

"How does one scrape together a sum like that, Jeeves?"

"It will call for thrift, m'lord."

"You bet it will. It'll take years."

"And Captain Biggar struck me as an impatient gentleman."

"You needn't rub it in, Jeeves."

"Very good, m'lord."

"Let's keep our minds on the present."

"Yes, m'lord. Remember that man's life lies all within this present, as 'twere but a hair's breadth of time. As for the rest, the past is gone, the future yet unseen."

"Eh?"

"Marcus Aurelius, m'lord."

"Oh? Well, as I was saying, let us glue our minds on what is going to happen if this Biggar suddenly blows in here. Do you think he'll recognize me?"

"I am inclined to fancy not, m'lord. The moustache and the patch formed a very effective disguise. After all, in the past few months we have encountered several gentlemen of your lordship's acquaintance——"

"And not one of them spotted me."

"No, m'lord. Nevertheless, facing the facts, I fear we must regard this afternoon's episode as a set-back. It is clearly impossible for us to function at the Derby tomorrow."

"I was looking forward to cleaning up on the Derby."

"I, too, m'lord. But after what has occurred, one's entire turf activities must, I fear, be regarded as suspended indefinitely."

"You don't think we could risk one more pop?"

"No, m'lord."

"I see what you mean, of course. Show up at Epsom tomorrow, and the first person we'd run into would be this Captain Biggar——"

"Straddling, like Apollyon, right across the way. Precisely, m'lord."

Bill passed a hand through his disordered hair.

"If only I had frozen on to the money we made at Newmarket!"

"Yes, m'lord. Of all sad words of tongue or pen the saddest are these—It might have been. Whittier."

"You warned me not to let our capital fall too low."

"I felt that we were not equipped to incur any heavy risk. That was why I urged your lordship so vehemently to lay Captain Biggar's second wager off. I had misgivings. True, the probability of the double bearing fruit at such odds was not great, but when I saw Whistler's Mother pass us on her way to the starting-post, I was conscious of a tremor of uneasiness. Those long legs, that powerful rump . . ."

"Don't, Jeeves!"

"Very good, m'lord."

"I'm trying not to think of Whistler's Mother."

"I quite understand, m'lord."

"Who the dickens *was* Whistler, anyway?"

"A figure, landscape and portrait painter of considerable distinction, m'lord, born in Lowell, Massachusetts, in 1834. His 'Portrait of my Mother', painted in 1872, is particularly esteemed by the *cognoscenti* and was purchased by the French Government for the Luxembourg Gallery, Paris, in 1892. His works are individual in character and notable for subtle colour harmony."

Bill breathed a little stertorously.

"It's subtle, is it?"

"Yes, m'lord."

"I see. Thanks for telling me. I was worrying myself sick about his colour harmony." Bill became calmer. "Jeeves, if the worst comes to the worst and Biggar does catch me bending, can I gain a bit of time by pleading the Gaming Act?"

"I fear not, m'lord. You took the gentleman's money. A cash transaction."

"It would mean choky, you feel?"

"I fancy so, m'lord."

"Would you be jugged, too, as my clerk?"

"In all probability, m'lord. I am not quite certain on the point. I should have to consult my solicitor."

"But I would be for it?"

"Yes, m'lord. The sentences, however, are not, I believe, severe."

"But think of the papers. The ninth Earl of Rowcester, whose ancestors held the field at Agincourt, skipped from the field at Epsom with a slavering punter after him. It'll be jam for the newspaper boys."

"Unquestionably the circumstance of your lordship having gone into business as a Silver Ring bookmaker would be accorded wide publicity."

Bill, who had been pacing the floor again, stopped in mid-stride and regarded the speaker with an accusing eye.

"And who was it suggested that I should go into business as a Silver Ring bookie? You, Jeeves. I don't want to be harsh, but you must own that the idea came from you. You were the——"

"*Fons et origo mali*, m'lord? That, I admit, is true. But if your lordship will recall, we were in something of a quandary. We had agreed that your lordship's impending marriage made it essential to augment your lordship's slender income, and we went through the Classified Trades section of the telephone directory in quest of a possible profession which your lordship might adopt. It was merely because nothing of a suitable nature had presented itself by the time we reached the T's that I suggested Turf Accountant *faute de mieux*."

"*Faute de* what?"

"*Mieux*, m'lord. A French expression. We should say 'for want of anything better'."

"What asses these Frenchmen are! Why can't they talk English?"

"They are possibly more to be pitied than censured, m'lord. Early upbringing no doubt has a good deal to do with it. As I was saying, it seemed to me a happy solution of your lordship's difficulties. In the United States of America, I believe, bookmakers are considered persons of a somewhat low order and are, indeed, suppressed by the police, but in England it is very different. Here they are looked up to and courted. There is a school of thought which regards them as the new aristocracy. They make a great deal of money, and have the added gratification of not paying income-tax."

Bill sighed wistfully.

"*We* made a lot of money up to Newmarket."

"Yes, m'lord."

"And where is it now?"

"Where, indeed, m'lord?"

"I shouldn't have spent so much doing up the place."

"No, m'lord."

"And it was a mistake to pay my tailor's bill."

"Yes, m'lord. One feels that your lordship did somewhat overdo it there. As the old Roman observed, *ne quid nimis*."

"Yes, that was rash. Still, no good beefing about it now, I suppose."

"No, m'lord. The moving finger writes, and having writ——"

"Hoy!"

"——moves on, nor all your piety and wit can lure it back to cancel half a line nor all your tears wash out one word of it. You were saying, m'lord?"

"I was only going to ask you to cheese it."

"Certainly, m'lord."

"Not in the mood."

"Quite so, m'lord. It was only the appositeness of the quotation —from the works of the Persian poet Omar Khayyám—that led me to speak. I wonder if I might ask a question, m'lord?"

"Yes, Jeeves?"

"Is Miss Wyvern aware of your lordship's professional connection with the turf?"

Bill quivered like an aspen at the mere suggestion.

"I should say not. She would throw fifty-seven fits if she knew. I've rather given her the idea that I'm employed by the Agricultural Board."

"A most respectable body of men."

"I didn't actually say so in so many words. I just strewed the place with Agricultural Board report forms and took care she saw them. Did you know that they issue a hundred and seventy-nine different blanks other than the seventeen questionnaires?"

"No, m'lord. I was not aware. It shows zeal."

"Great zeal. They're on their toes, those boys."

"Yes, m'lord."

"But we're wandering from the point, which is that Miss Wyvern must never learn the awful truth. It would be fatal. At the outset of our betrothal she put her foot down firmly on the subject of my tendency to have an occasional flutter, and I promised her faithfully that I would never punt again. Well, you might argue that being a Silver Ring bookie is not the same thing as punting, but I doubt if you would ever sell that idea to Miss Wyvern."

"The distinction is certainly a nice one, m'lord."

"Let her discover the facts, and all would be lost."

"Those wedding bells would not ring out."

"They certainly wouldn't. She would return me to store before I could say 'What ho'. So if she comes asking questions, reveal nothing. Not even if she sticks lighted matches between your toes."

"The contingency is a remote one, m'lord."

"Possibly. I'm merely saying, whatever happens, Jeeves, secrecy and silence."

"You may rely on me, m'lord. In the inspired words of Pliny the Younger——"

Bill held up a hand. "Right ho, Jeeves."

"Very good, m'lord."

"I'm not interested in Pliny the Younger."

"No, m'lord."

"As far as I'm concerned, you may take Pliny the Younger and put him where the monkey put the nuts."

"Certainly, m'lord."

"And now leave me, Jeeves. I have a lot of heavy brooding to do. Go and get me a stiffish whisky and soda."

"Very good, m'lord. I will attend to the matter immediately."

Jeeves melted from the room with a look of respectful pity, and Bill sat down and put his head between his hands. A hollow groan escaped him, and he liked the sound of it and gave another.

He was starting on a third, bringing it up from the soles of his feet, when a voice spoke at his side.

"Good heavens, Bill. What on earth's the matter?"

Jill Wyvern was standing there.

★ 5 ★

I N the interval which had elapsed since her departure from the living room, Jill had rubbed American ointment on Mike the Irish terrier, taken a look at a goldfish belonging to the cook, which had caused anxiety in the kitchen by refusing its ants' eggs, and made a routine tour of the pigs and cows, giving one of the latter a bolus. She had returned to the house agreeably conscious of duty done and looking forward to a chat with her loved one, who, she presumed, would by now be back from his Agricultural Board rounds and in a mood for pleasant dalliance. For even when the Agricultural Board know they have got hold of an exceptionally good man and wish (naturally) to get every possible ounce of work out of him, they are humane enough to let the poor peon call it a day round about the hour of the evening cocktail.

To find him groaning with his head in his hands was something of a shock.

"What on earth's the matter?" she repeated.

Bill had sprung from his chair with a convulsive leap. That loved voice, speaking unexpectedly out of the void when he supposed himself to be alone with his grief, had affected him like a buzz-saw applied to the seat of his trousers. If it had been Captain C. G. Brabazon-Biggar, of the United Rovers Club, Northumberland Avenue, he could not have been much more perturbed. He gaped at her, quivering in every limb. Jeeves, had he been present, would have been reminded of Macbeth seeing the ghost of Banquo.

"Matter?" he said, inserting three m's at the beginning of the word.

Jill was looking at him with grave, speculative eyes. She had that direct, honest gaze which many nice girls have, and as a rule Bill liked it. But at the moment he could have done with something that did not pierce quite so like a red-hot gimlet to his inmost soul. A sense of guilt makes a man allergic to direct, honest gazes.

"Matter?" he said, getting the word shorter and crisper this time. "What do you mean, what's the matter? Nothing's the matter. Why do you ask?"

"You were groaning like a foghorn."

"Oh, that. Touch of neuralgia."

"You've got a headache?"

"Yes, it's been coming on some time. I've had rather an exhausting afternoon."

"Why, aren't the crops rotating properly? Or are the pigs going in for smaller families?"

"My chief problem today," said Bill dully, "concerned horses."

A quick look of suspicion came into Jill's gaze. Like all nice girls, she had, where the man she loved was concerned, something of the Private Eye about her.

"Have you been betting again?"

Bill stared.

"*Me?*"

"You gave me your solemn promise you wouldn't. Oh, Bill, you are an idiot. You're more trouble to look after than a troupe of performing seals. Can't you see it's just throwing money away? Can't you get it into your fat head that the punters haven't a hope against the bookmakers? I know people are always talking about bringing off fantastic doubles and winning thousands of pounds with a single fiver, but that sort of thing never really happens. What did you say?"

Bill had not spoken. The sound that had proceeded from his twisted lips had been merely a soft moan like that of an emotional red Indian at the stake.

"It happens sometimes," he said hollowly. "I've heard of cases."

"Well, it couldn't happen to you. Horses just aren't lucky for you."

Bill writhed. The illusion that he was being roasted over a slow fire had become extraordinarily vivid.

"Yes," he said, "I see that now."

Jill's gaze became more direct and penetrating than ever.

"Come clean, Bill. Did you back a loser in the Oaks?"

This was so diametrically opposite to what had actually occurred that Bill perked up a little.

"Of course I didn't."

"You swear?"

"I may begin to at any moment."

"You didn't back anything in the Oaks?"

"Certainly not."

"Then what's the matter?"

"I told you. I've got a headache."

"Poor old thing. Can I get you anything?"

"No, thanks. Jeeves is bringing me a whisky and soda."

"Would a kiss help, while you're waiting?"

"It would save a human life."

Jill kissed him, but absently. She appeared to be thinking.

"Jeeves was with you today, wasn't he?" she said.

"Yes. Yes, Jeeves was along."

"You always take him with you on these expeditions of yours."

"Yes."

"Where do you go?"

"We make the rounds."

"Doing what?"

"Oh, this and that."

"I see. How's the headache?"

"A little better, thanks."

"Good."

There was silence for a moment.

"I used to have headaches a few years ago," said Jill.

"Bad?"

"Quite bad. I suffered agonies."

"They do touch you up, don't they?"

"They do. But," proceeded Jill, her voice rising and a hard note creeping into her voice, "my headaches, painful as they were, never made me look like an escaped convict lurking in a bush listening to the baying of the bloodhounds and wondering every minute when the hand of doom was going to fall on the seat of his pants. And that's how you are looking now. There's guilt written on your every feature. If you were to tell me at this moment that you had done a murder and were worrying because you had suddenly remembered you hadn't hidden the body properly, I would say 'I thought as much'. Bill, for the last time, what's the matter?"

"Nothing's the matter."

"Don't tell me."

"I am telling you."

"There's nothing on your mind?"

"Not a thing."

"You're as gay and carefree as a lark singing in the summer sky?"

"If anything, rather more so."

There was another silence. Jill was biting her lip, and Bill wished she wouldn't. There is, of course, nothing actually low and degrading in a girl biting her lip, but it is a spectacle that a *fiancé* with a good deal on his mind can never really enjoy.

"Bill, tell me," said Jill. "How do you feel about marriage?"

Bill brightened. This, he felt, was more the stuff.

"I think it's an extraordinarily good egg. Always provided, of course, that the male half of the sketch is getting someone like you."

"Never mind the pretty speeches. Shall I tell you how I feel about it?"

"Do."

"I feel that unless there is absolute trust between a man and a girl, they're crazy even to think of getting married, because if they're going to hide things from each other and not tell each other their troubles, their marriage is bound to go on the rocks sooner or later. A husband and wife ought to tell each other everything. I wouldn't ever dream of keeping anything from you, and if it interests you to know it, I'm as sick as mud to think that you're keeping this trouble of yours, whatever it is, from me."

"I'm not in any trouble."

"You are. What's happened, I don't know, but a short-sighted mole that's lost its spectacles could see that you're a soul in torment. When I came in here, you were groaning your head off."

Bill's self-control, so sorely tried today, cracked.

"Damn it all," he bellowed, "why shouldn't I groan? I believe Rowcester Abbey is open for being groaned in at about this hour, is it not? I wish to heaven you would leave me alone," he went on, gathering momentum. "Who do you think you are? One of these G-men fellows questioning some rat of the Underworld? I suppose you'll be asking next where I was on the night of February the twenty-first. Don't be such an infernal Nosy Parker."

Jill was a girl of spirit, and with girls of spirit this sort of thing soon reaches saturation point.

"I don't know if you know it," she said coldly, "but when you spit on your hands and get down to it, you can be the world's premier louse."

"That's a nice thing to say."

"Well, it's the truth," said Jill. "You're simply a pig in human shape. And if you want to know what I think," she went on, gathering momentum in her turn, "I believe what's happened is that you've gone and got mixed up with some awful female."

"You're crazy. Where the dickens could I have met any awful females?"

"I should imagine you have had endless opportunities. You're always going off in your car, sometimes for a week at a stretch. For all I know, you may have been spending your time festooned with hussies."

"I wouldn't so much as look at a hussy if you brought her to me on a plate with watercress round her."

"I don't believe you."

"And it was you, if memory serves me aright," said Bill, "who some two and a half seconds ago were shooting off your head about the necessity for absolute trust between us. Women!" said Bill bitterly. "Women! My God, what a sex!"

On this difficult situation Jeeves entered, bearing a glass on a salver.

"Your whisky and soda, m'lord," he said, much as a President of the United States might have said to a deserving citizen 'Take this Congressional medal'.

Bill accepted the restorative gratefully.

"Thank you, Jeeves. Not a moment before it was needed."

"And Sir Roderick and Lady Carmoyle are in the yew alley, asking to see you, m'lord."

"Good heavens! Rory and the Moke? Where did they spring from? I thought she was in Jamaica."

"Her ladyship returned this morning, I understand, and Sir Roderick obtained compassionate leave from Harrige's in order to accompany her here. They desired me to inform your lordship that they would be glad of a word with you at your convenience before the arrival of Mrs. Spottsworth."

"Before the what of who? Who on earth's Mrs. Spottsworth?"

"An American lady whose acquaintance her ladyship made in New York, m'lord. She is expected here this evening. I gathered from what her ladyship and Sir Roderick were saying that there is some prospect of Mrs. Spottsworth buying the house."

Bill gaped.

"Buying the house?"

"Yes, m'lord."

"*This* house?"

"Yes, m'lord."

"Rowcester Abbey, you mean?"

"Yes, m'lord."

"You're pulling my leg, Jeeves."

"I would not take such a liberty, m'lord."

"You seriously mean that this refugee from whatever American loony-bin it was where she was under observation until she sneaked out with false whiskers on is actually contemplating paying hard cash for Rowcester Abbey?"

"That was the interpretation which I placed on the remarks of her ladyship and Sir Roderick, m'lord."

Bill drew a deep breath.

"Well, I'll be blowed. It just shows you that it takes all sorts to make a world. Is she coming to stay?"

"So I understood, m'lord."

"Then you might remove the two buckets you put to catch the water under the upper hall skylight. They create a bad impression."

"Yes, m'lord. I will also place some more drawing pins in the wallpaper. Where would your lordship be thinking of depositing Mrs. Spottsworth?"

"She'd better have the Queen Elizabeth room. It's the best we've got."

"Yes, m'lord. I will insert a wire screen in the flue to discourage intrusion by the bats that nest there."

"We can't give her a bathroom, I'm afraid."

"I fear not, m'lord."

"Still, if she can make do with a shower, she can stand under the upper hall skylight."

Jeeves pursed his lips.

"If I might offer the suggestion, m'lord, it is not judicious to speak in that strain. Your lordship might forget yourself and let fall some such observation in the hearing of Mrs. Spottsworth."

Jill, standing at the French window and looking out with burning eyes, had turned and was listening, electrified. The generous wrath which had caused her to allude to her betrothed as a pig in human shape had vanished completely. It could not compete with this stupendous news. As far as Jill was concerned, the war was over.

She thoroughly concurred with Jeeves's rebuke.

"Yes, you poor fish," she said. "You mustn't even think like that. Oh, Bill, isn't it wonderful! If this comes off, you'll have money enough to buy a farm. I'm sure we'd do well running a farm, me as a vet and you with all your expert farming knowledge."

"My what?"

Jeeves coughed.

"I think Miss Wyvern is alluding to the fact that you have had such wide experience working for the Agricultural Board, m'lord."

"Oh, ah, yes. I see what you mean. Of course, yes, the Agricultural Board. Thank you, Jeeves."

"Not at all, m'lord."

Jill developed her theme.

"If you could sting this Mrs. Spottsworth for something really big, we could start a prize herd. That pays like anything. I wonder how much you could get for the place."

"Not much, I'm afraid. It's seen better days."

"What are you going to ask?"

"Three thousand and five pounds two shillings and sixpence."

"What!"

Bill blinked.

"Sorry. I was thinking of something else."

"But what put an odd sum like that into your head?"

"I don't know."

"You must know."

"I don't."

"But you must have had some *reason*."

"The sum in question arose in the course of his lordship's work in connection with his Agricultural Board duties this afternoon, miss," said Jeeves smoothly. "Your lordship may recall that I observed at the time that it was a peculiar figure."

"So you did, Jeeves, so you did."

"That was why your lordship said 'Three thousand and five pounds two shillings and sixpence'."

"Yes, that was why I said 'Three thousand and five pounds two shillings and sixpence'."

"These momentary mental aberrations are not uncommon, I believe. If I might suggest it, m'lord, I think it would be advisable to proceed to the yew alley without further delay. Time is of the essence."

"Of course, yes. They're waiting for me, aren't they? Are you coming, Jill?"

"I can't, darling. I have patients to attend to. I've got to go all the way over to Stover to see the Mainwarings' Peke, though I don't suppose there's the slightest thing wrong with it. That dog is the worst hypochondriac."

"Well, you're coming to dinner all right?"

"Of course. I'm counting the minutes. My mouth's watering already."

Jill went out through the French window. Bill mopped his forehead. It had been a near thing.

"You saved me there, Jeeves," he said. "But for your quick thinking all would have been discovered."

"I am happy to have been of service, m'lord."

"Another instant, and womanly intuition would have been doing its stuff, with results calculated to stagger humanity. You eat a lot of fish, don't you, Jeeves?"

"A good deal, m'lord."

"So Bertie Wooster has often told me. You sail into the sole and sardines like nobody's business, he says, and he attributes your giant intellect to the effects of the phosphorus. A hundred times, he says, it has enabled you to snatch him from the soup at the eleventh hour. He raves about your great gifts."

"Mr. Wooster has always been gratifyingly appreciative of my humble efforts on his behalf, m'lord."

"What beats me and has always beaten me is why he ever let you go. When you came to me that day and said you were at liberty, you could have bowled me over. The only explanation I could think of was that he was off his rocker . . . or more off his rocker than he usually is. Or did you have a row with him and hand in your portfolio?"

Jeeves seemed distressed at the suggestion.

"Oh, no, m'lord. My relations with Mr. Wooster continue uniformly cordial, but circumstances have compelled a temporary separation. Mr. Wooster is attending a school which does not permit its student body to employ gentlemen's personal gentlemen."

"A school?"

"An institution designed to teach the aristocracy to fend for itself, m'lord. Mr. Wooster, though his finances are still quite sound, feels that it is prudent to build for the future, in case the social revolution should set in with even greater severity. Mr. Wooster . . . I can hardly mention this without some display of emotion . . . is actually learning to darn his own socks. The course he is taking includes boot-cleaning, sock-darning, bed-making and primary grade cooking."

"Golly! Well, that's certainly a novel experience for Bertie."

"Yes, m'lord. Mr. Wooster doth suffer a sea change into something rich and strange. I quote the Bard of Stratford. Would your lordship care for another quick whisky and soda before joining Lady Carmoyle?"

"No, we mustn't waste a moment. As you were saying not long ago, time is of the . . . what, Jeeves?"

"Essence, m'lord."

"Essence? You're sure?"

"Yes, m'lord."

"Well, if you say so, though I always thought an essence was a sort of scent. Right ho, then, let's go."

"Very good, m'lord."

6

IT was with her mind in something of a whirl that Mrs. Spottsworth had driven away from the door of the Goose and Gherkin. The encounter with Captain C. G. Biggar had stirred her quite a good deal.

Mrs. Spottsworth was a woman who attached considerable importance to what others of less sensitivity would have dismissed carelessly as chance happenings or coincidences. She did not believe in chance. In her lexicon there was no such word as coincidence. These things, she held, were *meant*. This unforeseen return into her life of the White Hunter could be explained, she felt, only on the supposition that some pretty adroit staff work had been going on in the spirit world.

It had happened at such a particularly significant moment. Only two days previously A. B. Spottsworth, chatting with her on the ouija board, had remarked, after mentioning that he was very happy and eating lots of fruit, that it was high time she thought of getting married again. No sense, A. B. Spottsworth had said, in her living a lonely life with all that money in the bank. A woman needs a mate, he had asserted, adding that Cliff Bessemer, with whom he had exchanged a couple of words that morning in the vale of light, felt the same. 'And they don't come more level-headed than old Cliff Bessemer,' said A. B. Spottsworth.

And when his widow had asked 'But, Alexis, wouldn't you and Clifton *mind* me marrying again?' A. B. Spottsworth had replied in his bluff way, spelling the words out carefully, 'Of course we wouldn't, you dumb-bell. Go to it, kid.'

And right on top of that dramatic conversation who should pop up out of a trap but the man who had loved her with a strong silent passion from the first moment they had met. It was uncanny. One would have said that passing the veil made the late Messrs. Bessemer and Spottsworth clairvoyant.

Inasmuch as Captain Biggar, as we have seen, had not spoken his love but had let concealment like a worm i' the bud feed on his tomato-coloured cheek, it may seem strange that Mrs. Spottsworth should have known anything about the way he felt. But a woman can always tell. When she sees a man choke up and look like an embarrassed beetroot every time he catches her eye over the eland steaks and lime-juice, she soon forms an adequate diagnosis of his case.

The recurrence of these phenomena during those moments of farewell outside the Goose and Gherkin showed plainly, moreover, that the passage of time had done nothing to cool off the gallant Captain. She had not failed to observe the pop-eyed stare in his keen blue eyes, the deepening of the hue of his vermilion face and the way his number eleven feet had shuffled from start to finish of the interview. If he did not still consider her the tree on which the fruit of his life hung, Rosalinda Spottsworth was vastly mistaken. She was a little surprised that nothing had emerged in the way of an impassioned declaration. But how could she know that a feller had his code?

Driving through the pleasant Southmoltonshire country, she found her thoughts dwelling lingeringly on Captain C. G. Biggar.

At their very first meeting in Kenya she had found something about him that attracted her, and two days later this mild liking had become a rather fervent admiration. A woman cannot help but respect a man capable of upping with his big-bored .505 Gibbs and blowing the stuffing out of a charging buffalo. And from respect to love is as short a step as that from Harrige's Glass, Fancy Goods and Chinaware department to the Ladies' Underclothing. He seemed to her like someone out of Ernest Hemingway, and she had always had a weakness for those rough, tough devil-may-care Hemingway characters. Spiritual herself, she was attracted by roughness and toughness in the male. Clifton Bessemer had had those qualities. So had A. B. Spottsworth. What had first impressed her in Clifton Bessemer had been the way he had swatted a charging fly with a rolled-up evening paper at the studio party where they had met, and in the case of A. B. Spottsworth the spark had been lit when she heard him one afternoon in conversation with a Paris taxi-driver who had expressed dissatisfaction with the amount of his fare.

As she passed through the great gates of Rowcester Abbey and made her way up the long drive, it was beginning to seem to her that she might do considerably worse than cultivate Captain Biggar. A woman needs a protector, and what better protector can she find than a man who thinks nothing of going into tall grass after a wounded lion? True, wounded lions do not enter largely into the ordinary married life, but it is nice for a wife to know that, if one does happen to come along, she can leave it with every confidence to her husband to handle.

It would not, she felt, be a difficult matter to arrange the necessary preliminaries. A few kind words and a melting look or two ought to be quite sufficient to bring that strong, passionate nature to the boil. These men of the wilds respond readily to melting looks.

She was just trying one out in the mirror of her car when, as she rounded a bend in the drive, Rowcester Abbey suddenly burst upon her view, and for the moment Captain Biggar was forgotten. She could think of nothing but that she had found the house of her dreams. Its mellow walls aglow in the rays of the setting sun, its windows glittering like jewels, it seemed to her like some palace of Fairyland. The little place in Pasadena, the little place in Carmel, and the little places in New York, Florida, Maine and Oregon were well enough in their way, but this outdid them all. Houses like Rowcester Abbey always look their best from outside and at a certain distance.

She stopped the car and sat there, gazing raptly.

Rory and Monica, tired of waiting in the yew alley, had returned to the house and met Bill coming out. All three had gone back into the living-room, where they were now discussing the prospects of a quick sale to this female Santa Claus from across the Atlantic. Bill, though feeling a little better after his whisky and soda, was still in a feverish state. His goggling eyes and twitching limbs would have interested a Harley Street physician, had one been present to observe them.

"Is there a hope?" he quavered, speaking rather like an invalid on a sick bed addressing his doctor.

"I think so," said Monica.

"I don't," said Rory.

Monica quelled him with a glance.

"The impression I got at that women's lunch in New York," she said, "was that she was nibbling. I gave her quite a blast of propaganda and definitely softened her up. All that remains now is to administer the final shove. When she arrives, I'll leave you alone together, so that you can exercise that well-known charm of yours. Give her the old personality."

"I will," said Bill fervently. "I'll be like a turtle dove cooing to a female turtle-dove. I'll play on her as on a stringed instrument."

"Well, mind you do, because if the sale comes off, I'm expecting a commission."

"You shall have it, Moke, old thing. You shall be repaid a thousandfold. In due season there will present themselves at your front door elephants laden with gold and camels bearing precious stones and rare spices."

"How about apes, ivory and peacocks?"

"They'll be there."

Rory, the practical, hard-headed business man, frowned on this visionary stuff.

"Well, will they?" he said. "The point seems to me extremely moot. Even on the assumption that this woman is weak in the head I can't see her paying a fortune for a place like Rowcester Abbey. To start with, all the farms are gone."

"That's true," said Bill, damped. "And the park belongs to the local golf club. There's only the house and garden."

"The garden, yes. And we know all about the garden, don't we? I was saying to Moke only a short while ago that whereas in the summer months the river is at the bottom of the garden——"

"Oh, be quiet," said Monica. "I don't see why you shouldn't get fifteen thousand pounds, Bill. Maybe even as much as twenty."

Bill revived like a watered flower.

"Do you really think so?"

"Of course she doesn't," said Rory. "She's just trying to cheer you up, and very sisterly of her, too. I honour her for it. Under that forbidding exterior there lurks a tender heart. But twenty thousand quid for a house from which even Reclaimed Juvenile Delinquents recoil in horror? Absurd. The thing's a relic of the past. A hundred and forty-seven rooms!"

"That's a lot of house," argued Monica.

"It's a lot of junk," said Rory firmly. "It would cost a bally fortune to do it up."

Monica was obliged to concede this.

"I suppose so," she said. "Still, Mrs. Spottsworth's the sort of woman who would be quite prepared to spend a million or so on that. You've been making a few improvements, I notice," she said to Bill.

"A drop in the bucket."

"You've even done something about the smell on the first-floor landing."

"Wish I had the money it cost."

"You're hard up?"

"Stony."

"Then where the dickens," said Rory, pouncing like a prosecuting counsel, "do all these butlers and housemaids come from? That girl Jill Stick-in-the-mud——"

"Her name is not Stick-in-the-mud."

Rory raised a restraining hand.

"Her name may or may not be Stick-in-the-mud," he said, letting the point go, for after all it was a minor one, "but the fact remains that she was holding us spellbound just now with a description of your domestic amenities which suggested the mad luxury that led to the fall of Babylon. Platoons of butlers, beauty choruses of housemaids, cooks in reckless profusion and stories flying about of boys to clean the knives and boots. . . . I said to Moke after she'd left that I wondered if you had set up as a gentleman bur . . . That reminds me, old girl. Did you tell Bill about the police?"

Bill leaped a foot, and came down shaking in every limb.

"The police? What about the police?"

"Some blighter rang up from the local gendarmerie. The rozzers want to question you."

"What do you mean, question me?"

"Grill you," explained Rory. "Give you the third degree. And there was another call before that. A mystery man who didn't give his name. He and Moke kidded back and forth for a while."

"Yes, I talked to him," said Monica. "He had a voice that sounded as if he ate spinach with sand in it. He was inquiring about the licence number of your car."

"What!"

"You haven't run into somebody's cow, have you? I understand that's a very serious offence nowadays."

Bill was still quivering briskly.

"You mean someone was wanting to know the licence number of my car?"

"That's what I said. Why, what's the matter, Bill? You're looking as worried as a prune."

"White and shaken," agreed Rory. "Like a side-car." He laid a kindly hand on his brother-in-law's shoulder. "Bill, tell me. Be frank. Why are you wanted by the police?"

"I'm not wanted by the police'"

"Well, it seems to be their dearest wish to get their hands on you. One theory that crossed my mind," said Rory, "was—I mentioned it to you, Moke, if you remember—that you had found some opulent bird with a guilty secret and were going in for a spot of blackmail. This may or may not be the case, but if it is, now is the time to tell us, Bill, old man. You're among friends. Moke's broadminded, and I'm broadminded. I know the police look a bit squiggle-eyed at blackmail, but I can't see any objection to it myself. Quick profits and practically no overheads. If I had a son, I'm not at all sure I wouldn't have him trained for that profession. So if the flatties are after you and you would like a helping hand to get you out of the country before they start watching the ports, say the word, and we'll . . ."

"Mrs. Spottsworth," announced Jeeves from the doorway, and a moment later Bill had done another of those leaps in the air which had become so frequent with him of late.

He stood staring pallidly at the vision that entered.

7

Mrs. SPOTTSWORTH had come sailing into the room with the confident air of a woman who knows that her hat is right, her dress is right, her shoes are right and her stockings are right and that she has a matter of forty-two million dollars tucked away in sound securities, and Bill, with a derelict country house for sale, should have found her an encouraging spectacle. For unquestionably she looked just the sort of person who would buy derelict English country houses by the gross without giving the things a second thought.

But his mind was not on business transactions. It had flitted back a few years and was in the French Riviera, where he and this woman had met and—he could not disguise it from himself—become extremely matey.

It had all been perfectly innocent, of course—just a few moonlight drives, one or two mixed bathings and hob-nobbings at Eden Roc and the ordinary exchanges of civilities customary on the French Riviera—but it seemed to him that there was a grave danger of her introducing into their relations now that touch of Auld Lang Syne which is the last thing a young man wants when he has a fiancée around—and a fiancée, moreover, who has already given evidence of entertaining distressing suspicions.

Mrs. Spottsworth had come upon him as a complete and painful surprise. At Cannes he had got the impression that her name was Bessemer, but of course in places like Cannes you don't bother much about surnames. He had, he recalled, always addressed her as Rosie, and she—he shuddered—had addressed him as Billiken. A clear, but unpleasant, picture rose before his eyes of Jill's face when she heard her addressing him as Billiken at dinner tonight. Most unfortunately, through some oversight, he had omitted to mention to Jill his Riviera acquaintance Mrs. Bessemer, and he could see that she might conceivably take a little explaining away.

"How nice to see you again, Rosalinda," said Monica. "So glad you found your way here all right. It's rather tricky after you leave the main road. My husband, Sir Roderick Carmoyle. And this is——"

"Billiken!" cried Mrs. Spottsworth, with all the enthusiasm of a generous nature. It was plain that if the ecstasy occasioned by this unexpected encounter was a little one-sided, on her side at least it existed in full measure.

"Eh?" said Monica.

"Mr. Belfry and I are old friends. We knew each other in Cannes a few years ago, when I was Mrs. Bessemer."

"Bessemer!"

"It was not long after my husband had passed the veil owing to having a head-on collision with a truck full of beer bottles on the Jericho Turnpike. His name was Clifton Bessemer."

Monica shot a pleased and congratulatory look at Bill. She knew all about Mrs. Bessemer of Cannes. She was aware that her brother had given this Mrs. Bessemer the rush of a lifetime, and what better foundation could a young man with a house to sell have on which to build.

"Well, that's fine," she said. "You'll have all sorts of things to talk about, won't you? But he isn't Mr. Belfry now, he's Lord Rowcester."

"Changed his name," explained Rory. "The police are after him, and an *alias* was essential."

"Oh, don't be an ass, Rory. He came into the title," said Monica. "You know how it is in England. You start out as something, and then someone dies and you do a switch. Our uncle, Lord Rowcester, pegged out not long ago, and Bill was his heir, so he shed the Belfry and took on the Rowcester."

"I see. Well, to me he will always be Billiken. How are you, Billiken?"

Bill found speech, though not much of it and what there was rather rasping.

"I'm fine, thanks—er—Rosie."

"Rosie?" said Rory, startled and, like the child of nature he was, making no attempt to conceal his surprise. "Did I hear you say Rosie?"

Bill gave him a cold look.

"Mrs. Spottsworth's name, as you have already learned from a usually well-informed source—viz. Moke—is Rosalinda. All her friends—even casual acquaintances like myself—called her Rosie."

"Oh, ah," said Rory. "Quite, quite. Very natural, of course."

"Casual acquaintances?" said Mrs. Spottsworth, pained.

Bill plucked at his tie.

"Well, I mean blokes who just knew you from meeting you at Cannes and so forth."

"Cannes!" cried Mrs. Spottsworth ecstatically. "Dear, sunny, gay, delightful Cannes! What times we had there, Billiken! Do you remember——"

"Yes, yes," said Bill. "Very jolly, the whole thing. Won't you have a drink or a sandwich or a cigar or something?"

Fervently he blessed the Mainwarings' Peke for being so confirmed a hypochondriac that it had taken Jill away to the other side of the county. By the time she returned, Mrs. Spottsworth, he trusted, would have simmered down and become less expansive on the subject of the dear old days. He addressed himself to the task of curbing her exuberance.

"Nice to welcome you to Rowcester Abbey," he said formally.

"Yes, I hope you'll like it," said Monica.

"It's the most wonderful place I ever saw!"

"Would you say that? Mouldering old ruin, I'd call it," said Rory judicially, and was fortunate enough not to catch his wife's eye, "Been decaying for centuries. I'll bet if you shook those curtains, a couple of bats would fly out."

"The patina of Time!" said Mrs. Spottsworth. "I adore it." She closed her eyes. " 'The dead, twelve deep, clutch at you as you go by'," she murmured.

"What a beastly idea," said Rory. "Even a couple of clutching corpses would be a bit over the odds, in my opinion."

Mrs. Spottsworth opened her eyes. She smiled.

"I'm going to tell you something very strange," she said. "It struck me so strongly when I came in at the front door I had to sit down for a moment. Your butler thought I was ill."

"You aren't, I hope?"

"No, not at all. It was simply that I was . . . overcome. I realized that I had been here before."

Monica looked politely puzzled. It was left to Rory to supply the explanation.

"Oh, as a sightseer?" he said. "One of the crowd that used to come on Fridays during the summer months to be shown over the place at a bob a head. I remember them well in the days when you and I were walking out, Moke. The Gogglers, we used to call them. They came in charabancs and dropped nut chocolate on the carpets. Not that dropping nut chocolate on them would make these carpets any worse. That's all been discontinued now, hasn't it, Bill? Nothing left to goggle at, I suppose. The late Lord Rowcester," he explained to the visitor, "stuck the Americans with all his best stuff, and now there's not a thing in the place worth looking at. I was saying to my wife only a short while ago that by far the best policy in dealing with Rowcester Abbey would be to burn it down."

A faint moan escaped Monica. She raised her eyes heavenwards, as if pleading for a thunderbolt to strike this man. If this was her Roderick's idea of selling goods to a customer, it seemed a miracle that he had ever managed to get rid of a single hose-pipe, lawn-mower or bird-bath.

Mrs. Spottsworth shook her head with an indulgent smile.

"No, no, I didn't mean that I had been here in my present corporeal envelope. I meant in a previous incarnation. I'm a Rotationist, you know."

Rory nodded intelligently.

"Ah, yes. Elks, Shriners and all that. I've seen pictures of them, in funny hats."

"No, no, you are thinking of Rotarians. I am a Rotationist, which is quite different. We believe that we are reborn as one of our ancestors every ninth generation."

"Ninth?" said Monica, and began to count on her fingers.

"The mystic ninth house. Of course you've read the *Zend Avesta of Zoroaster*, Sir Roderick?"

"I'm afraid not. Is it good?"

"Essential, I would say."

"I'll put it on my library list," said Rory. "By Agatha Christie, isn't it?"

Monica had completed her calculations.

"Ninth . . . That seems to make me Lady Barbara, the leading hussy of Charles the Second's reign."

Mrs. Spottsworth was impressed.

"I suppose I ought to be calling you Lady Barbara and asking you about your latest love affair."

"I only wish I could remember it. From what I've heard of her, it would make quite a story."

"Did she get herself sunburned all over?" asked Rory. "Or was she more of an indoor girl?"

Mrs. Spottsworth had closed her eyes again.

"I feel influences," she said. "I even hear faint whisperings. How strange it is, coming into a house that you last visited three hundred years ago. Think of all the lives that have been lived within these ancient walls. And they are here, all around us, creating an intriguing aura for this delicious old house."

Monica caught Bill's eye.

"It's in the bag, Bill," she whispered.

"Eh?" said Rory in a loud, hearty voice. "What's in the bag?"

"Oh, shut up."

"But what *is* in the . . . Ouch!" He rubbed a well-kicked ankle. "Oh, ah, yes, of course. Yes, I see what you mean."

Mrs. Spottsworth passed a hand across her brow. She appeared to be in a sort of mediumistic trance.

"I seem to remember a chapel. There is a chapel here?"

"Ruined," said Monica.

"You don't need to tell her that, old girl," said Rory.

"I knew it. And there's a Long Gallery."

"That's right," said Monica. "A duel was fought in it in the eighteenth century. You can still see the bullet holes in the walls."

"And dark stains on the floor, no doubt. This place must be full of ghosts."

This, felt Monica, was an idea to be discouraged at the outset.

"Oh, no, don't worry," she said heartily. "Nothing like that in Rowcester Abbey," and was surprised to observe that her guest was gazing at her with large, woebegone eyes like a child informed that the evening meal will not be topped off with ice-cream.

"But I want ghosts," said Mrs. Spottsworth. "I must have ghosts. Don't tell me there aren't *any*?"

Rory was his usual helpful self.

"There's what we call the haunted lavatory on the ground floor," he said. "Every now and then, when there's nobody near it, the toilet will suddenly flush, and when a death is expected in the family, it justs keeps going and going. But we don't know if it's a spectre or just a defect in the plumbing."

"Probably a poltergeist," said Mrs. Spottsworth, seeming a little disappointed. "But are there no visual manifestations?"

"I don't think so."

"Don't be silly, Rory," said Monica. "Lady Agatha."

Mrs. Spottsworth was intrigued.

"Who was Lady Agatha?"

"The wife of Sir Caradoc the Crusader. She has been seen several times in the ruined chapel."

"Fascinating, fascinating," said Mrs. Spottsworth. "And now

let me take you to the Long Gallery. Don't tell me where it is. Let me see if I can't find it for myself."

She closed her eyes, pressed her finger-tips to her temples, paused for a moment, opened her eyes and started off. As she reached the door, Jeeves appeared.

"Pardon me, m'lord."

"Yes, Jeeves?"

"With reference to Mrs. Spottsworth's dog, m'lord, I would appreciate instructions as to meal hours and diet."

"Pomona is very catholic in her tastes," said Mrs. Spottsworth. "She usually dines at five, but she is not at all fussy."

"Thank you, madam."

"And now I must concentrate. This is a test." Mrs. Spottsworth applied her finger-tips to her temple once more. "Follow, please, Monica. You, too, Billiken. I am going to take you straight to the Long Gallery."

The procession passed through the door, and Rory, having scrutinized it in his slow, thorough way, turned to Jeeves with a shrug of the shoulders.

"Potty, what?"

"The lady does appear to diverge somewhat from the generally accepted norm, Sir Roderick."

"She's as crazy as a bed bug. I'll tell you something, Jeeves. That sort of thing wouldn't be tolerated at Harrige's."

"No, sir?"

"Not for a moment. If this Mrs. Dogsbody, or whatever her name is, came into—say the Cakes, Biscuits and General Confectionery and started acting that way, the store detectives would have her by the seat of the trousers and be giving her the old heave-ho before the first gibber had proceeded from her lips."

"Indeed, Sir Roderick?"

"I'm telling you, Jeeves. I had an experience of that sort myself shortly after I joined. I was at my post one morning—I was in the Jugs, Bottles and Picnic Supplies at the time—and a woman came in. Well dressed, refined aspect, nothing noticeable about her at all except that she was wearing a fireman's helmet—I started giving her courteous service. 'Good morning, madam,' I said. 'What can I do for you, madam? Something in picnic supplies, madam? A jug? A bottle?' She looked at me keenly. 'Are you interested in bottles, gargoyle?' she asked, addressing me for some reason as gargoyle. 'Why, yes, madam,' I replied. 'Then what do you think of this one,' she said. And with that she whipped out a whacking great decanter and brought it whizzing down on the exact spot where my frontal bone would have been, had I not started back like a nymph surprised while bathing. It shattered itself on the counter. It was enough. I beckoned to the store detectives and they scooped her up."

"Most unpleasant, Sir Roderick."

"Yes, shook me, I confess. Nearly made me send in my papers. It turned out that she had recently been left a fortune by a wealthy uncle in Australia, and it had unseated her reason. This Mrs. Dogsbody's trouble is, I imagine, the same. Inherited millions from a platoon of deceased husbands, my wife informs me, and took advantage of the fact to go right off her onion. Always a mistake, Jeeves, unearned money. There's nothing like having to scratch for a living. I'm twice the man I was since I joined the ranks of the world's workers."

"You see eye to eye with the Bard, Sir Roderick. 'Tis deeds must win the prize."

"Exactly. Quite so. And speaking of winning prizes, what about tomorrow?"

"Tomorrow, Sir Roderick?"

"The Derby. Know anything?"

"I fear not, Sir Roderick. It would seem to be an exceptionally open contest. Monsieur Boussac's Voleur is, I understand, the favourite. Fifteen to two at last night's call-over and the price likely to shorten to sixes or even fives for the S.P. But the animal in question is somewhat small and lightly boned for so gruelling an ordeal. Though we have, to be sure, seen such a handicap overcome. The name of Manna, the 1925 winner, springs to the mind, and Hyperion, another smallish horse, broke the course record previously held by Flying Fox, accomplishing the distance in two minutes, thirty-four seconds."

Rory regarded him with awe.

"By Jove! You know your stuff, don't you?"

"One likes to keep *au courant* in these matters, sir. It is, one might say, an essential part of one's education."

"Well, I'll certainly have another chat with you tomorrow before I put my bet on."

"I shall be most happy if I can be of service, Sir Roderick," said Jeeves courteously, and oozed softly from the room, leaving Rory with the feeling, so universal among those who encountered this great man, that he had established connection with some wise, kindly spirit in whose hands he might place his affairs without a tremor.

A few moments later, Monica came in, looking a little jaded.

"Hullo, old girl," said Rory. "Back from your travels? Did she find the ruddy Gallery?"

Monica nodded listlessly.

"Yes, after taking us all over the house. She said she lost the influence for a while. Still, I suppose it wasn't bad after three hundred years."

"I was saying to Jeeves a moment ago that the woman's as crazy as a bed bug. Though, arising from that, how is it that bed bugs have got their reputation for being mentally unbalanced? Now that she's over in this country, I expect she'll soon be receiving all sorts of flattering offers from Colney Hatch and similar establishments. What became of Bill?"

"He didn't stay the course. He disappeared. Went to dress, I suppose."

"What sort of state was he in?"

"Glassy-eyed and starting at sudden noises."

"Ah, still jittery. He's certainly got the jumps all right, our William. But I've had another theory about old Bill," said Rory. "I don't think his nervousness is due to his being one jump ahead of the police. I now attribute it to his having got this job with the Agricultural Board and, like all these novices, pitching in too strenuously at first. We fellows who aren't used to work have got to learn to husband our strength, to keep something in reserve, if you know what I mean. That's what I'm always preaching to the chaps under me. Most of them listen, but there's one lad—in the Midgets Outfitting—you've never seen such *drive*. That boy's going to burn himself out before he's fifty. Hullo, whom have we here?"

He stared, at a loss, at a tall, good-looking girl who had just entered. A momentary impression that this was the ghost of Lady Agatha, who, wearying of the ruined chapel, had come to join the party, he dismissed. But he could not place her. Monica saw more clearly into the matter. Observing the cap and apron, she deduced that this must be that almost legendary figure, the housemaid.

"Ellen?" she queried.

"Yes, m'lady. I was looking for his lordship."

"I think he's in his room. Anything I can do?"

"It's this gentleman that's just come, asking to see his lordship, m'lady. I saw him driving up in his car and, Mr. Jeeves being busy in the dining-room, I answered the door and showed him into the morning-room."

"Who is he?"

"A Captain Biggar, m'lady."

Rory chuckled amusedly.

"Biggar? Reminds me of that game we used to play when we were kids, Moke—the Bigger Family."

"I remember."

"You do? Then which is bigger, Mr. Bigger or Mrs. Bigger?"

"Rory, really."

"Mr. Bigger, because he's father Bigger. Which is bigger, Mr. Bigger or his old maid aunt?"

"You're not a child now, you know."

"Can you tell me, Ellen?"

"No, sir."

"Perhaps Mrs. Dogsbody can," said Rory, as that lady came bustling in.

There was a look of modest triumph on Mrs. Spottsworth's handsome face.

"Did you tell Sir Roderick?" she said.

"I told him," said Monica.

"I found the Long Gallery, Sir Roderick."

"Three rousing cheers," said Rory. "Continue along these lines, and you'll soon be finding bass drums in telephone booths. But pigeon-holing that for the moment, do you know which is bigger, Mr. Bigger or his old maid aunt?"

Mrs. Spottsworth looked perplexed.

"I beg your pardon?"

Rory repeated his question, and her perplexity deepened.

"But I don't understand."

"Rory's just having one of his spells," said Monica.

"The old maid aunt," said Rory, "because, whatever happens, she's always Bigger."

"Pay no attention to him," said Monica. "He's quite harmless on these occasions. It's just that a Captain Biggar has called. That set him off. He'll be all right in a minute."

Mrs. Spottsworth's fine eyes had widened.

"Captain Biggar?"

"There's another one," said Rory, knitting his brow, "only it eludes me for the moment. I'll get it soon. Something about Mr. Biggar and his son."

"Captain Biggar?" repeated Mrs. Spottsworth. She turned to Ellen. "Is he a gentleman with a rather red face?"

"He's a gentleman with a very red face," said Ellen. She was a girl who liked to get these things right.

Mrs. Spottsworth put a hand to her heart.

"How extraordinary!"

"You know him?" said Monica.

"He is an old, old friend of mine. I knew him when . . . Oh, Monica, could you . . . would you . . . could you possibly invite him to stay?"

Monica started like a war-horse at the sound of the bugle.

"Why, of course, Rosalinda. Any friend of yours. What a splendid idea."

"Oh, thank you." Mrs. Spottsworth turned to Ellen. "Where is Captain Biggar?"

"In the morning-room, madam."

"Will you take me there at once. I must see him."

"If you will step this way, madam."

Mrs. Spottsworth hurried out, followed sedately by Ellen. Rory shook his head dubiously.

"Is this wise, Moke, old girl? Probably some frightful outsider in a bowler hat and a made-up tie."

Monica's eyes were sparkling.

"I don't care what he's like. He's a friend of Mrs. Spottsworth's, that's all that matters. Oh, Bill!" she cried, as Bill came in.

Bill was tail-coated, white-tied and white-waistcoated, and his hair gleamed with strange unguents. Rory stared at him in amazement.

"Good God, Bill! You look like Great Lovers Through The Ages. If you think I'm going to dress up like that, you're much mistaken. You get the old Carmoyle black tie and soft shirt, and like it. I get the idea, of course. You've dolled yourself up to impress Mrs. Spottsworth and bring back memories of the old days at Cannes. But I'd be careful not to overdo it, old boy. You've got to consider Jill. If she finds out about you and the Spottsworth——"

Bill started.

"What the devil do you mean?"

"Nothing, nothing. I was only making a random remark."

"Don't listen to him, Bill," said Monica. "He's just drooling. Jill's sensible."

"And after all," said Rory, looking on the bright side, "it all happened before you met Jill."

"All what happened?"

"Nothing, old boy, nothing."

"My relations with Mrs. Spottsworth were pure to the last drop."

"Of course, of course."

"Do you sell muzzles at Harrige's, Rory?" asked Monica.

"Muzzles? Oh, rather. In the Cats, Dogs and Domestic Pets."

"I'm going to buy one for you, to keep you quiet. Just treat him as if he wasn't there, Bill, and listen while I tell you the news. The most wonderful thing has happened. An old friend of Mrs. Spottsworth's has turned up, and I've invited him to stay."

"An old friend?"

"Another old lover, one presumes."

"Do stop it, Rory. Can't you understand what a marvellous thing this is, Bill! We've put her under an obligation. Think what a melting mood she'll be in after this!"

Her enthusiasm infected Bill. He saw just what she meant.

"You're absolutely right. This is terrific."

"Yes, isn't it a stroke of luck? She'll be clay in your hands now."

"Clay is the word. Moke, you're superb. As fine a bit of quick thinking as I ever struck. Who is the fellow?"

"His name's Biggar. Captain Biggar."

Bill groped for support at a chair. A greenish tinge had spread over his face.

"What!" he cried. "Captain B-b-b——?"

"Ha!" said Rory. "Which is bigger, Mr. Bigger or Master Bigger? Master Bigger, because he's a little Bigger. I knew I'd get it," he said complacently.

8

I T was a favourite dictum of the late A. B. Spottsworth, who, though fond of his wife in an absent-minded sort of way, could never have been described as a ladies' man or mistaken for one of those Troubadours of the Middle Ages, that the secret of a happy and successful life was to get rid of the women at the earliest possible opportunity. Give the gentler sex the bum's rush, he used to say, removing his coat and reaching for the poker chips, and you could start to go places. He had often observed that for sheer beauty and uplift few sights could compare with that of the female members of a dinner-party filing out of the room at the conclusion of the meal, leaving the men to their soothing masculine conversation.

To Bill Rowcester at nine o'clock on the night of this disturbing day such an attitude of mind would have seemed incomprehensible. The last thing in the world that he desired was Captain Biggar's soothing masculine conversation. As he stood holding the dining-room door open while Mrs. Spottsworth, Monica and Jill passed through on their way to the living-room, he was weighed down by a sense of bereavement and depression, mingled with uneasy speculations as to what was going to happen now. His emotions, in fact, were similar in kind and intensity to those which a garrison beleaguered by savages would have experienced, had the United States Marines, having arrived, turned right round and walked off in the opposite direction.

True, all had gone perfectly well so far. Even he, conscience-stricken though he was, had found nothing to which he could take exception in the Captain's small talk up till now. Throughout dinner, starting with the soup and carrying on to the sardines on toast, the White Hunter had confined himself to such neutral topics as cannibal chiefs he had met and what to do when cornered by head-hunters armed with poisoned blowpipes. He had told two rather long and extraordinarily dull stories about a couple of friends of his called Tubby Frobisher and the Subahdar. And he had recommended to Jill, in case she should ever find herself in need of one, an excellent ointment for use when bitten by alligators. To fraudulent bookmakers, chases across country and automobile licences he had made no reference whatsoever.

But now that the women had left and two strong men—or three, if you counted Rory—stood face to face, who could say how long this happy state of things would last? Bill could but trust that Rory would not bring the conversation round to the dangerous subject by asking the Captain if he went in for racing at all.

"Do you go in for racing at all, Captain?" said Rory as the door closed.

A sound rather like the last gasp of a dying zebra shot from Captain Biggar's lips. Bill, who had risen some six inches into the air, diagnosed it correctly as a hollow, mirthless laugh. He had had some idea of uttering something along those lines himself.

"Racing?" Captain Biggar choked. "Do I go in for racing at all? Well, mince me up and smother me in onions!"

Bill would gladly have done so. Such a culinary feat would, it seemed to him, have solved all his perplexities. He regretted that the idea had not occurred to one of the cannibal chiefs of whom his guest had been speaking.

"It's the Derby Dinner tonight," said Rory. "I'll be popping along shortly to watch it on the television set in the library. All the top owners are coming on the screen to say what they think of their chances tomorrow. Not that the blighters know a damn thing about it, of course. Were you at the Oaks this afternoon by any chance?"

Captain Biggar expanded like one of those peculiar fish in Florida which swell when you tickle them.

"Was I at the Oaks? *Chang suark!* Yes, sir, I was. And if ever a man——"

"Rather pretty, this Southmoltonshire country, don't you think, Captain?" said Bill. "Picturesque, as it is sometimes called. The next village to us—Lower Snodsbury—you may have noticed it as you came through—has a——"

"If ever a man got the ruddy sleeve across the bally wind-pipe," proceeded the Captain, who had now become so bright red that it was fortunate that by a lucky chance there were no bulls present in the dining-room, "it was me at Epsom this afternoon. I passed through the furnace like Shadrach, Meshach and Nebuchadnezzar or whoever it was. I had my soul tied up in knots and put through the wringer."

Rory tut-tutted sympathetically.

"Had a bad day, did you?"

"Let me tell you what happened."

"—Norman church," continued Bill, faint but persevering, "which I believe is greatly——"

"I must begin by saying that since I came back to the old country, I have got in with a pretty shrewd lot of chaps, fellows who know one end of a horse from the other, as the expression is, and they've been putting me on to some good things. And today——"

"—admired by blokes who are fond of Norman churches," said Bill. "I don't know much about them myself, but according to the nibs there's a nave or something on that order——"

Captain Biggar exploded again.

"Don't talk to me about knaves! *Yogi tulsiram jaginath!* I met the king of them this afternoon, blister his insides. Well, as I was saying, these chaps of mine put me on to good things from time to time, and today they advised a double. Lucy Glitters in the two-thirty and Whistler's Mother for the Oaks."

"Extraordinary, Whistler's Mother winning like that," said Rory. "The consensus of opinion at Harrige's was that she hadn't a hope."

"And what happened? Lucy Glitters rolled in at a hundred to six, and Whistler's Mother, as you may have heard, at thirty-three to one."

Rory was stunned. "You mean your double came off?"

"Yes, sir."

"At those odds?"

"At those odds."

"How much did you have on?"

"Five pounds on Lucy Glitters and all to come on Whistler's Mother's nose."

Rory's eyes bulged.

"Good God! Are you listening to this, Bill? You must have won a fortune."

"Three thousand pounds."

"Well, I'll be . . . Did you hear that, Jeeves?"

Jeeves had entered, bearing coffee. His deportment was, as ever, serene. Like Bill, he found Captain Biggar's presence in the home disturbing, but where Bill quaked and quivered, he continued to resemble a well-bred statue.

"Sir?"

"Captain Biggar won three thousand quid on the Oaks."

"Indeed, sir? A consummation devoutly to be wished."

"Yes," said the Captain sombrely. "Three thousand pounds I won, and the bookie did a bolt."

Rory stared. "No!"

"I assure you."

"Skipped by the light of the moon?"

"Exactly."

Rory was overcome.

"I never heard anything so monstrous. Did you ever hear anything so monstrous, Jeeves? Wasn't that the frozen limit, Bill?"

Bill seemed to come out of a trance.

"Sorry, Rory, I'm afraid I was thinking of something else. What were you saying?"

"Poor old Biggar brought off a double at Epsom this afternoon, and the swine of a bookie legged it, owing him three thousand pounds."

Bill was naturally aghast. Any good-hearted young man would have been, hearing such a story.

"Good heavens, Captain," he cried, "what a terrible thing to have happened. Legged it, did he, this bookie?"

"Popped off like a jack rabbit, with me after him."

"I don't wonder you're upset. Scoundrels like that ought not to be at large. It makes one's blood boil to think of this . . . this . . . what would Shakespeare have called him, Jeeves?"

"This arrant, rascally, beggarly, lousy knave, m'lord."

"Ah, yes. Shakespeare put these things well."

"A whoreson, beetle-headed, flap-eared knave, a knave, a rascal, an eater of broken meats; a beggarly, filthy, worsted-stocking——"

"Yes, yes, Jeeves, quite so. One gets the idea." Bill's manner was a little agitated. "Don't run away, Jeeves. Just give the fire a good stir."

"It is June, m'lord."

"So it is, so it is. I'm all of a doodah, hearing this appalling story. Won't you sit down, Captain? Oh, you are sitting down. The cigars, Jeeves. A cigar for Captain Biggar."

The Captain held up a hand.

"Thank you, no. I never smoke when I'm after big game."

"Big game? Oh, I see what you mean. This bookie fellow.

You're a White Hunter, and now you're hunting white bookies," said Bill with a difficult laugh. "Rather good, that, Rory?"

"Dashed good, old boy. I'm convulsed. And now may I get down? I want to go and watch the Derby Dinner."

"An excellent idea," said Bill heartily. "Let's all go and watch the Derby Dinner. Come along, Captain."

Captain Biggar made no move to follow Rory from the room. He remained in his seat, looking redder than ever.

"Later, perhaps," he said curtly. "At the moment, I would like to have a word with you, Lord Rowcester."

"Certainly, certainly, certainly, certainly, certainly," said Bill, though not blithely. "Stick around, Jeeves. Lots of work to do in here. Polish an ashtray or something. Give Captain Biggar a cigar."

"The gentleman has already declined your lordship's offer of a cigar."

"So he has, so he has. Well, well!" said Bill. "Well, well, well, well, well!" He lit one himself with a hand that trembled like a tuning-fork. "Tell us more about this bookie of yours, Captain."

Captain Biggar brooded darkly for a moment. He came out of the silence to express a wistful hope that some day it might be granted to him to see the colour of the fellow's insides.

"I only wish," he said, "that I could meet the rat in Kuala Lumpur."

"Kuala Lumpur?"

Jeeves was his customary helpful self.

"A locality in the Straits Settlements, m'lord, a British Crown Colony in the East Indies including Malacca, Penang and the province of Wellesley, first made a separate dependency of the British Crown in 1853 and placed under the Governor-General of India. In 1887 the Cocos or Keeling Islands were attached to the colony, and in 1889 Christmas Island. Mr. Somerset Maugham has written searchingly of life in those parts."

"Of course, yes. It all comes back to me. Rather a strange lot of birds out there, I gather."

Captain Biggar conceded this.

"A very strange lot of birds. But we generally manage to put salt on their tails. Do you know what happens to a welsher in Kuala Lumpur, Lord Rowcester?"

"No, I—er—don't believe I've ever heard. Don't go, Jeeves. Here's an ashtray you've missed. What does happen to a welsher in Kuala Lumpur?"

"We let the blighter have three days to pay up. Then we call on him and give him a revolver."

"That's rather nice of you. Sort of heaping coals of . . . You don't mean a *loaded* revolver?"

"Loaded in all six chambers. We look the louse in the eye, leave the revolver on the table and go off. Without a word. He understands."

Bill gulped. The strain of the conversation was beginning to tell on him.

"You mean he's expected to . . . Isn't that a bit drastic?"

Captain Biggar's eyes were cold and hard, like picnic eggs.

"It's the code, sir. Code! That's a big word with the men who live on the frontiers of Empire. Morale can crumble very easily out there. Drink, women and unpaid gambling debts, those are the steps down," he said. "Drink, women and unpaid gambling debts," he repeated, illustrating with jerks of the hand.

"That one's the bottom, is it? You hear that, Jeeves?"

"Yes, m'lord."

"Rather interesting."

"Yes, m'lord."

"Broadens the mind a bit."

"Yes, m'lord."

"One lives and learns, Jeeves."

"One does indeed, m'lord."

Captain Biggar took a Brazil nut, and cracked it with his teeth.

"We've got to set an example, we bearers of the white man's burden. Can't let the Dyaks beat us on code."

"Do they try?"

"A Dyak who defaults on a debt has his head cut off."

"By the other Dyaks?"

"Yes, sir, by the other Dyaks."

"Well, well."

"The head is then given to his principal creditor."

This surprised Bill. Possibly it surprised Jeeves, too, but Jeeves' was a face that did not readily register such emotions as astonishment. Those who knew him well claimed on certain occasions of great stress to have seen a very small muscle at the corner of his mouth give one quick, slight twitch, but as a rule his features preserved a uniform imperturbability, like those of a cigar-store Indian.

"Good heavens!" said Bill. "You couldn't run a business that way over here. I mean to say, who would decide who was the principal creditor? Imagine the arguments there would be, Eh, Jeeves?"

"Unquestionably, m'lord. The butcher, the baker . . ."

"Not to mention hosts who had entertained the Dyak for weekends, from whose houses he had slipped away on Monday morning, forgetting the Saturday night bridge game."

"In the event of his surviving, it would make such a Dyak considerably more careful in his bidding, m'lord."

"True, Jeeves, true. It would, wouldn't it? He would think twice about trying any of that psychic stuff?"

"Precisely, m'lord. And would undoubtedly hesitate before taking his partner out of a business double."

Captain Biggar cracked another nut. In the silence it sounded like one of those explosions which slay six.

"And now," he said, "with your permission, I would like to cut the *ghazi havildar* and get down to brass tacks, Lord Rowcester." He paused a moment, marshalling his thoughts. "About this bookie."

Bill blinked.

"Ah, yes, this bookie. I know the bookie you mean."

"For the moment he has got away, I am sorry to say. But I had the sense to memorize the number of his car."

"You did? Shrewd, Jeeves."

"Very shrewd, m'lord."

"I then made inquiries of the police. And do you know what they told me? They said that that car number, Lord Rowcester, was yours."

Bill was amazed. "Mine?"

"Yours."

"But how could it be mine?"

"That is the mystery which we have to solve. This Honest Patch Perkins, as he called himself, must have borrowed your car . . . with or without your permission."

"Incredulous!"

"Incredible, m'lord."

"Thank you, Jeeves. Incredible! How would I know any Honest Patch Perkins?"

"You don't?"

"Never heard of him in my life. Never laid eyes on him. What does he look like?"

"He is tall . . . about your height . . . and wears a ginger moustache and a black patch over his left eye."

"No, dash it, that's not possible . . . Oh, I see what you mean. A black patch over his left eye and a ginger moustache on the upper lip. I thought for a moment . . ."

"And a check coat and a crimson tie with blue horse-shoes on it."

"Good heavens! He must look the most ghastly outsider. Eh, Jeeves?"

"Certainly far from *soigné*, m'lord."

"Very far from *soigné*. Oh, by the way, Jeeves, that reminds me. Bertie Wooster told me that you once made some such remark to him, and it gave him the idea for a ballad to be entitled 'Way down upon the *soigné* river'. Did anything ever come of it, do you know?"

"I fancy not, m'lord'"

"Bertie wouldn't have been equal to whacking it out, I suppose, But one can see a song hit there, handled by the right person."

"No doubt, m'lord."

"Cole Porter could probably do it."

"Quite conceivably, m'lord."

"Or Oscar Hammerstein."

"It should be well within the scope of Mr. Hammerstein's talents, m'lord."

It was with a certain impatience that Captain Biggar called the meeting to order.

"To hell with song hits and Cole Porters!" he said, with an abruptness on which Emily Post would have frowned. "I'm not talking about Cole Porter, I'm talking about this bally bookie who was using your car today."

Bill shook his head.

"My dear old pursuer of pumas and what-have-you, you say you're talking about bally bookies, but what you omit to add is that you're talking through the back of your neck. Neat that, Jeeves."

"Yes, m'lord. Crisply put."

"Obviously what happened was that friend Biggar got the wrong number."

"Yes, m'lord."

The red of Captain Biggar's face deepened to purple. His proud spirit was wounded.

"Are you telling me I don't know the number of a car that I

followed all the way from Epsom Downs to Southmoltonshire? That car was used today by this Honest Patch Perkins and his clerk, and I'm asking you if you lent it to him."

"My dear good bird, would I lend my car to a chap in a check suit and a crimson tie, not to mention a black patch and a ginger moustache? The thing's not ... what, Jeeves?"

"Feasible, m'lord." Jeeves coughed. "Possibly the gentleman's eyesight needs medical attention."

Captain Biggar swelled portentously.

"My eyesight? *My* eyesight? Do you know who you're talking to? I am Bwana Biggar."

"I regret that the name is strange to me, sir. But I still maintain that you have made the pardonable mistake of failing to read the licence number correctly."

Before speaking again, Captain Biggar was obliged to swallow once or twice, to restore his composure. He also took another nut.

"Look," he said, almost mildly. "Perhaps you're not up on these things. You haven't been told who's who and what's what. I am Biggar the White Hunter, the most famous White Hunter in all Africa and Indonesia. I can stand without a tremor in the path of an onrushing rhino ... and why? Because my eyesight is so superb that I know ... I *know* I can get him in that one vulnerable spot before he has come within sixty paces. That's the sort of eyesight mine is."

Jeeves maintained his iron front.

"I fear I cannot recede from my position, sir. I grant that you may have trained your vision for such a contingency as you have described, but, poorly informed as I am on the subject of the larger fauna of the East, I do not believe that rhinoceri are equipped with licence numbers."

It seemed to Bill that the time had come to pour oil on the troubled waters and dish out a word of comfort.

"This bookie of yours, Captain. I think I can strike a note of hope. We concede that he legged it with what appears to have been the swift abandon of a bat out of hell, but I believe that when the fields are white with daisies he'll pay you. I get the impression that he's simply trying to gain time."

"I'll give him time," said the Captain morosely. "I'll see that he gets plenty. And when he has paid his debt to Society, I shall attend to him personally. A thousand pities we're not out East. They understand these things there. If they know you for a straight shooter and the other chap's a wrong 'un . . . well, there aren't many questions asked."

Bill started like a frightened fawn.

"Questions about what?"

" 'Good riddance' sums up their attitude. The fewer there are of such vermin, the better for Anglo-Saxon prestige."

"I suppose that's one way of looking at it."

"I don't mind telling you that there are a couple of notches on my gun that aren't for buffaloes . . . or lions . . . or elands . . . *or* rhinos."

"Really? What are they for?"

"Cheaters."

"Ah, yes. Those are those leopard things that go as fast as race-horses."

Jeeves had a correction to make.

"Somewhat faster, m'lord. A half-mile in forty-five seconds."

"Great Scott! Pretty nippy, what? That's travelling, Jeeves."

"Yes, m'lord."

"That's a cheetah, that was, as one might say."

Captain Biggar snorted impatiently.

"Chea-*ters* was what I said. I'm not talking about cheetah, the animal . . . though I have shot some of those, too."

"Too?"

"Too."

"I see," said Bill, gulping a little. "Too."

Jeeves coughed.

"Might I offer a suggestion, m'lord?"

"Certainly, Jeeves. Offer several."

"An idea has just crossed my mind, m'lord. It has occurred to me that it is quite possible that this racecourse character against whom Captain Biggar nurses a justifiable grievance may have sub-stituted for his own licence plate a false one——"

"By Jove, Jeeves, you've hit it!"

"—and that by some strange coincidence he selected for this false plate the number of your lordship's car."

"Exactly. That's the solution. Odd we didn't think of that before. It explains the whole thing, doesn't it, Captain?"

Captain Biggar was silent. His thoughtful frown told that he was weighing the idea.

"Of course it does," said Bill buoyantly. "Jeeves, your bulging brain, with its solid foundation of fish, has solved what but for you would have remained one of those historic mysteries you read about. If I had a hat on, I would raise it to you."

"I am happy to have given satisfaction, m'lord."

"You always do, Jeeves, you always do. It's what makes you so generally esteemed."

Captain Biggar nodded.

"Yes, I suppose that might have happened. There seems to be no other explanation."

"Jolly, getting these things cleared up," said Bill. "More port, Captain?"

"No, thank you."

"Then suppose we join the ladies. They're probably wondering what the dickens has happened to us and saying 'He cometh not', like . . . who, Jeeves?"

"Mariana of the Moated Grange, m'lord. Her tears fell with the dews at even; her tears fell ere the dews were dried. She could not look on the sweet heaven either at morn or eventide."

"Oh, well, I don't suppose our absence has hit them quite as hard as that. Still, it might be as well . . . Coming, Captain?"

"I should first like to make a telephone call."

"You can do it from the living-room."

"A private telephone call."

"Oh, right ho. Jeeves, conduct Captain Biggar to your pantry and unleash him on the instrument."

"Very good, m'lord."

Left alone, Bill lingered for some moments, the urge to join the ladies in the living-room yielding to a desire to lower just one more glass of port by way of celebration. Honest Patch Perkins had, he felt, rounded a nasty corner.

The only thought that came to mar his contentment had to do with Jill. He was not quite sure of his standing with that lodestar of his life. At dinner, Mrs. Spottsworth, seated on his right, had been chummy beyond his gloomiest apprehensions, and he fancied he had detected in Jill's eye one of those cold, pensive looks which are the last sort of look a young man in love likes to see in the eye of his betrothed.

Fortunately, Mrs. Spottsworth's chumminess had waned as the meal proceeded and Captain Biggar started monopolizing the conversation. She had stopped talking about the old Cannes days and had sat lingering in rapt silence as the White Hunter told of antres vast and deserts idle and of the cannibals that each other eat, the

Anthropophagi, and men whose heads do grow beneath their shoulders.

This to hear had Mrs. Spottsworth seriously inclined, completely switching off the Cannes motif, so it might be that all was well.

Jeeves returned, and he greeted him effusively as one who had fought the good fight.

"That was a brain wave of yours, Jeeves."

"Thank you, m'lord."

"It eased the situation considerably. His suspicions are lulled, don't you think?"

"One would be disposed to fancy so, m'lord."

"You know, Jeeves, even in these disturbed post-war days, with the social revolution turning handsprings on every side and Civilization, as you might say, in the melting-pot, it's still quite an advantage to be in big print in *Debrett's Peerage*."

"Unquestionably so, m'lord. It gives a gentleman a certain standing."

"Exactly. People take it for granted that you're respectable. Take an Earl, for instance. He buzzes about, and people say 'Ah, an Earl' and let it go at that. The last thing that occurs to them is that he may in his spare moments be putting on patches and false moustaches and standing on a wooden box in a check coat and a tie with blue horseshoes, shouting 'Five to one the field, bar one!'"

"Precisely, m'lord."

"A satisfactory state of things."

"Highly satisfactory, m'lord."

"There have been moments today, Jeeves, I don't mind confessing, when it seemed to me that the only thing to do was to turn up the toes and say 'This is the end', but now it would take very little to start me singing like the Cherubim and Seraphim. It was the Cherubim and Seraphim who sang, wasn't it?"

"Yes, m'lord. Hosanna, principally."

"I feel a new man. The odd sensation of having swallowed a quart of butterflies, which I got when there was a burst of red fire and a roll of drums from the orchestra and that White Hunter shot up through a trap at my elbow, has passed away completely."

"I am delighted to hear it, m'lord."

"I knew you would be, Jeeves, I knew you would be. Sympathy and understanding are your middle names. And now," said Bill, "to join the ladies in the living-room and put the poor souls out of their suspense."

9

ARRIVING in the living-room, he found that the number of ladies available for being joined there had been reduced to one—reading from left to right, Jill. She was sitting on the settee twiddling an empty coffee-cup and staring before her with what are sometimes described as unseeing eyes. Her air was that of a girl who is brooding on something, a girl to whom recent happenings have given much food for thought.

"Hullo there, darling," cried Bill with the animation of a ship-wrecked mariner sighting a sail. After that testing session in the dining-room, almost anything that was not Captain Biggar would have looked good to him, and she looked particularly good.

Jill glanced up.

"Oh, hullo," she said.

It seemed to Bill that her manner was reserved, but he proceeded with undiminished exuberance.

"Where's everybody?"

"Rory and Moke are in the library, looking in at the Derby Dinner."

"And Mrs. Spottsworth?"

"Rosie," said Jill in a toneless voice, "has gone to the ruined chapel. I believe she is hoping to get a word with the ghost of Lady Agatha."

Bill started. He also gulped a little.

"Rosie?"

"I think that is what you call her, is it not?"

"Why—er—yes."

"And she calls you Billiken. Is she a very old friend?"

"No, no. I knew her slightly at Cannes one summer."

"From what I heard her saying at dinner about moonlight drives and bathing from the Eden Roc, I got the impression that you had been rather intimate."

"Good heavens, no. She was just an acquaintance, and a pretty mere one, at that."

"I see."

There was a silence.

"I wonder if you remember," said Jill, at length breaking it, "what I was saying this evening before dinner about people not hiding things from each other, if they are going to get married?"

"Er—yes . . . Yes . . . I remember that."

"We agreed that it was the only way."

"Yes . . . Yes, that's right. So we did."

"I told you about Percy, didn't I? And Charles and Squiffy and Tom and Blotto," said Jill, mentioning other figures of Romance from the dead past. "I never dreamed of concealing the fact that I had been engaged before I met you. So why did you hide this Spottsworth from me?"

It seemed to Bill that, for a pretty good sort of chap who meant no harm to anybody and strove always to do the square thing by one and all, he was being handled rather roughly by Fate this summer day. The fellow—Shakespeare, he rather thought, though he would have to check with Jeeves—who had spoken of the slings and arrows of outrageous fortune, had known what he was talking about. Slings and arrows described it to a nicety.

"I didn't hide this Spottsworth from you!" he cried passionately. "She just didn't happen to come up. Lord love a duck, when you're sitting with the girl you love, holding her little hand and whispering words of endearment in her ear, you can't suddenly switch the conversation to an entirely different topic and say 'Oh, by the way, there was a woman I met in Cannes some years ago, on the subject of whom I would now like to say a few words. Let me tell you all about the time we drove to St. Tropez'."

"In the moonlight."

"Was it my fault that there was a moon? I wasn't consulted. And as for bathing from the Eden Roc, you talk as if we had had the ruddy Eden Roc to ourselves with not another human being in sight. It was not so, but far otherwise. Every time we took a dip, the water was alive with exiled Grand Dukes and stiff with dowagers of the most rigid respectability."

"I still think it odd you never mentioned her."

"I don't."

"I do. And I think it still odder that when Jeeves told you this afternoon that a Mrs. Spottsworth was coming here, you just said 'Oh, ah?' or something and let it go as if you had never heard the name before. Wouldn't the natural thing have been to say 'Mrs. Spottsworth? Well, well, bless my soul, I wonder if that can possibly be the woman with whom I was on terms of mere acquaintanceship at Cannes a year or two ago. Did I ever tell you about her, Jill? I used to drive with her a good deal in the moonlight, though of course in quite a distant way'."

It was Bill's moment.

"No," he thundered, "it would not have been the natural thing to say 'Mrs. Spottsworth? Well, well,' and so on and so forth, and I'll tell you why. When I knew her . . . slightly, as I say, as one does know people in places like Cannes . . . her name was Bessemer."

"Oh?"

"Precisely. B with an E with an S with an S with an E with an M with an E with an R. Bessemer. I have still to learn how all this Spottsworth stuff arose."

Jeeves came in. Duty called him at about this hour to collect the coffee-cups, and duty never called to this great man in vain.

His arrival broke what might be called the spell. Jill, who had more to say on the subject under discussion, withheld it. She got up and made for the French window.

"Well, I must be getting along," she said, still speaking rather tonelessly.

Bill stared.

"You aren't leaving already?"

"Only to go home and get some things. Moke has asked me to stay the night."

"Then Heaven bless Moke! Full marks for the intelligent female."

"You like the idea of my staying the night?"

"It's terrific."

"You're sure I shan't be in the way?"

"What on earth are you talking about? Shall I come with you?"

"Of course not. You're supposed to be a host."

She went out, and Bill, gazing after her fondly, suddenly stiffened. Like a delayed-action bomb, those words 'You're sure I shan't be in the way?' had just hit him. Had they been mere idle words? Or had they contained a sinister significance?

"Women are odd, Jeeves," he said.

"Yes, m'lord."

"Not to say peculiar. You can't tell what they mean when they say things, can you?"

"Very seldom, m'lord."

Bill brooded for a moment.

"Were you observing Miss Wyvern as she buzzed off?"

"Not closely, m'lord."

"Was her manner strange, do you think?"

"I could not say, m'lord. I was concentrating on coffee-cups."

Bill brooded again. This uncertainty was preying on his nerves. 'You're sure I shan't be in the way?' Had there been a nasty tinkle in her voice as she uttered the words? Everything turned on that. If no tinkle, fine. But if tinkle, things did not look so good. The question, plus tinkle, could only mean that his reasoned explanation of the Spottsworth-Cannes sequence had failed to get across and that she still harboured suspicions, unworthy of her though such suspicions might be.

The irritability which good men feel on these occasions swept over him. What was the use of being as pure as the driven snow, or possibly purer, if girls were going to come tinkling at you?"

"The whole trouble with women, Jeeves," he said, and the philosopher Schopenhauer would have slapped him on the back and told him he knew just how he felt, "is that practically all of them are dotty. Look at Mrs. Spottsworth. Wacky to the eyebrows. Roosting in a ruined chapel in the hope of seeing Lady Agatha."

"Indeed, m'lord? Mrs. Spottsworth is interested in spectres?"

"She eats them alive. Is that balanced behaviour?"

"Psychical research frequently has an appeal for the other sex, m'lord. My Aunt Emily——"

Bill eyed him dangerously.

"Remember what I said about Pliny the Younger, Jeeves?"

"Yes, m'lord."

"That goes for your Aunt Emily as well."

"Very good, m'lord."

"I'm not interested in your Aunt Emily."

"Precisely, m'lord. During her long lifetime very few people were."

"She is no longer with us?"

"No, m'lord."

"Oh, well, that's something," said Bill.

Jeeves floated out, and he flung himself into a chair. He was thinking once more of that cryptic speech, and now his mood had become wholly pessimistic. It was no longer any question of a tinkle or a non-tinkle. He was virtually certain that the words

'You're sure I shan't be in the way?' had been spoken through clenched teeth and accompanied by a look of infinite meaning. They had been the words of a girl who had intended to make a nasty crack.

He was passing his hands through his hair with a febrile gesture, when Monica entered from the library. She had found the celebrants at the Derby Dinner a little on the long-winded side. Rory was still drinking in every word, but she needed an intermission.

She regarded her hair-twisting brother with astonishment.

"Good heavens, Bill! Why the agony? What's up?

Bill glared unfraternally.

"Nothing's up, confound it! Nothing, nothing, nothing, nothing, nothing!"

Monica raised her eyebrows.

"Well, there's no need to be stuffy about it. I was only being the sympathetic sister."

With a strong effort Bill recovered the chivalry of the Rowcesters. "I'm sorry, Moke old thing. I've got a headache."

"My poor lamb!"

"It'll pass off in a minute."

"What you need is fresh air."

"Perhaps I do."

"And pleasant society. Ma Spottsworth's in the ruined chapel. Pop along and have a chat with her."

"What!"

Monica became soothing.

"Now don't be difficult, Bill. You know as well as I do how important it is to jolly her along. A flash of speed on your part now may mean selling the house. The whole idea was that on top of my sales talk you were to draw her aside and switch on the charm. Have you forgotten what you said about cooing to her like a turtle dove? Dash off this minute and coo as you have never cooed before."

For a long moment it seemed as though Bill, his frail strength taxed beyond its limit of endurance, was about to suffer something in the nature of spontaneous combustion. His eyes goggled, his face flushed, and burning words trembled on his lips. Then suddenly, as if Reason had intervened with a mild 'Tut, tut', he ceased to glare and his cheeks slowly resumed their normal hue. He had seen that Monica's suggestion was good and sensible.

In the rush and swirl of recent events, the vitally urgent matter ·

of pushing through the sale of his ancestral home had been thrust into the background of Bill's mind. It now loomed up for what it was, the only existing life preserver bobbing about in the sea of troubles in which he was immersed. Clutch it, and he was saved. When you sold houses, he reminded himself, you got deposits, paid cash down. Such a deposit would be sufficient to dispose of the Biggar menace, and if the only means of securing it was to go to Rosalinda Spottsworth and coo, then go and coo he must.

Simultaneously there came to him the healing thought that if Jill had gone home to provide herself with things for the night, it would be at least half an hour before she got back, and in half an hour a determined man can do a lot of cooing.

"Moke," he said, "you're right. My place is at her side."

He hurried out, and a moment later Rory appeared at the library door.

"I say, Moke," said Rory, "can you speak Spanish?"

"I don't know. I've never tried. Why?"

"There's a Spaniard or an Argentine or some such bird in there telling us about his horse in his native tongue. Probably a rank outsider, still one would have been glad to hear his views. Where's Bill? Don't tell me he's still in there with the White Man's Burden?"

"No, he came in here just now, and went out to talk to Mrs. Spottsworth."

"I want to confer with you about old Bill," said Rory. "Are we alone and unobserved?"

"Unless there's someone hiding in that dower chest. What about Bill?"

"There's something up, old girl, and it has to do with this chap Biggar. Did you notice Bill at dinner?"

"Not particularly. What was he doing? Eating peas with his knife?"

"No, but every time he caught Biggar's eye, he quivered like an Ouled Naïl stomach dancer. For some reason Biggar affects him like an egg-whisk. Why? That's what I want to know. Who is this mystery man? Why has he come here? What is there between him and Bill that makes Bill leap and quake and shiver whenever he looks at him? I don't like it, old thing. When you married me, you never said anything about fits in the family, and I consider I have been shabbily treated. I mean to say, it's a bit thick, going to all the trouble and expense of wooing and winning the girl you love, only to discover shortly after the honeymoon that you've become brother-in-law to a fellow with St. Vitus Dance."

Monica reflected.

"Come to think of it," she said, "I do remember, when I told him a Captain Biggar had clocked in, he seemed a bit upset. Yes, I distinctly recall a greenish pallor and a drooping lower jaw. And I came in here just now and found him tearing his hair. I agree with you. It's sinister."

"And I'll tell you something else," said Rory. "When I left the dining-room to go and look at the Derby Dinner, Bill was all for coming too. 'How about it?' he said to Biggar, and Biggar, looking very puff-faced, said 'Later, perhaps. At the moment, I would like a word with you, Lord Rowcester'. In a cold, steely voice, like a magistrate about to fine you a fiver for pinching a policeman's helmet on Boat Race night. And Bill gulped like a stricken bull pup and said 'Oh, certainly, certainly' or words to that effect. It sticks out a mile that this Biggar has got something on old Bill."

"But what could he possibly have on him?"

"Just the question I asked myself, my old partner of joys and sorrows, and I think I have the solution. Do you remember those stories one used to read as a kid? The *Strand Magazine* used to be full of them."

"Which stories?"

"Those idol's eye stories. The ones where a gang of blighters pop over to India to pinch the great jewel that's the eye of the idol. They get the jewel all right, but they chisel one of the blighters out of his share of the loot, which naturally makes him as sore as a gumboil, and years later he tracks the other blighters down one by one in their respectable English homes and wipes them out to the last blighter, by way of getting a bit of his own back. You mark my words, old Bill is being chivvied by this chap Biggar because he did him out of his share of the proceeds of the green eye of the little yellow god in the temple of Vishnu, and I shall be much surprised if we don't come down to breakfast tomorrow morning and find him weltering in his blood among the kippers and sausages with a dagger of Oriental design in the small of his back."

"Ass!"

"Are you addressing me?"

"I am, and with knobs on. Bill's never been farther east than Frinton."

"He's been to Cannes."

"Is Cannes east? I never know. But he's certainly never been within smelling distance of Indian idols' eyes."

"I didn't think of that," said Rory. "Yes, that, I admit, does weaken my argument to a certain extent." He brooded tensely. "Ha! I have it now. I see it all. The rift between Bill and Biggar is due to the baby."

"What on earth are you talking about? What baby?"

"Bill's, working in close collaboration with Biggar's daughter, the apple of Biggar's eye, a poor, foolish little thing who loved not wisely but too well. And if you are going to say that girls are all wise nowadays, I reply 'Not one brought up in the missionary school at Squalor Lumpit'. In those missionary schools they explain the facts of life by telling the kids about the bees and the flowers till the poor little brutes don't know which is which."

"For heaven's sake, Rory."

"Mark how it works out with the inevitability of Greek tragedy or whatever it was that was so bally inevitable. Girl comes to England, no mother to guide her, meets a handsome young Englishman, and what happens? The first false step. The remorse . . . too late. The little bundle. The awkward interview with Father. Father all steamed up. Curses a bit in some native dialect and packs his elephant gun and comes along to see old Bill. '*Caramba!*' as that Spaniard is probably saying at this moment on the television screen. Still, there's nothing to worry about. I don't suppose he can make him marry her. All Bill will have to do is look after the little thing's education. Send it to school and so on. If a boy, Eton. If a girl, Roedean."

"Cheltenham."

"Oh, yes. I'd forgotten you were an Old Cheltonian. The question now arises, should young Jill be told? It hardly seems fair to allow her to rush unwarned into marriage with a ripsnorting *roué* like William, Earl of Rowcester."

"Don't call Bill a ripsnorting *roué!*"

"It is how we should describe him at Harrige's."

"As a matter of fact, you're probably all wrong about Bill and Biggar. I know the poor boy's jumpy, but most likely it hasn't anything to do with Captain Biggar at all. It's because he's all on edge, wondering if Mrs. Spottsworth is going to buy the house. In which connection, Rory, you old fathead, can't you do something to help the thing along instead of bunging a series of spanners into the works?"

"I don't get your drift."

"I will continue snowing. Ever since Mrs. Spottsworth arrived, you've been doing nothing but point out Rowcester Abbey's defects. Be constructive."

"In what way, my queen?"

"Well, draw her attention to some of the good things there are in the place."

Rory nodded dutifully, but dubiously.

"I'll do my best," he said. "But I shall have very little raw material to work with. And now, old girl, I imagine that Spaniard will have blown over by this time, so let us rejoin the Derby diners. For some reason or other—why, one cannot tell—I've got a liking for a beast called Oratory."

10

Mrs. spottsworth had left the ruined chapel. After a vigil of some twenty-five minutes she had wearied of waiting for Lady Agatha to manifest herself. Like many very rich women, she tended to be impatient and to demand quick service. When in the mood for spectres, she wanted them hot off the griddle. Returning to the garden, she had found a rustic seat and was sitting there smoking a cigarette and enjoying the beauty of the night.

It was one of those lovely nights which occur from time to time in an English June, mitigating the rigours of the island summer and causing manufacturers of raincoats and umbrellas to wonder uneasily if they have been mistaken in supposing England to be an earthly Paradise for men of their profession.

A silver moon was riding in the sky, and a gentle breeze blew from the west, bringing with it the heart-stirring scent of stock and tobacco plant. Shy creatures of the night rustled in the bushes at her side and, to top the whole thing off, somewhere in the woods beyond the river a nightingale had begun to sing with the full-throated zest of a bird conscious of having had a rave notice from the poet Keats and only a couple of nights ago a star spot on the programme of the B.B.C.

It was a night made for romance, and Mrs. Spottsworth recognized it as such. Although in her *vers libre* days in Greenwich Village she had gone in almost exclusively for starkness and squalor, even then she had been at heart a sentimentalist. Left to herself, she would have turned out stuff full of moons, Junes, loves, doves, blisses and kisses. It was simply that the editors of the poetry magazines seemed to prefer rat-ridden tenements, the smell of cooking cabbage, and despair, and a girl had to eat.

Fixed now as solidly financially as any woman in America and freed from the necessity of truckling to the tastes of editors, she was able to take the wraps off her romantic self, and as she sat on the rustic seat, looking at the moon and listening to the nightingale, a stylist like the late Gustave Flaubert, tireless in his quest of the *mot juste*, would have had no hesitation in describing her mood as mushy.

To this mushiness Captain Biggar's conversation at dinner had contributed largely. We have given some indication of its trend, showing it ranging freely from cannibal chiefs to dart-blowing head-hunters, from head-hunters to alligators, and its effect on Mrs. Spottsworth had been very similar to that of Othello's reminiscences on Desdemona. In short, long before the last strawberry had been eaten, the final nut consumed, she was convinced that this was the mate for her and resolved to spare no effort in pushing the thing along. In the matter of marrying again, both A. B. Spottsworth and Clifton Bessemer had given her the green light, and there was consequently no obstacle in her path.

There appeared, however, to be one in the path leading to the rustic seat, for at this moment there floated to her through the silent night the sound of a strong man tripping over a flower-pot. It was followed by some pungent remarks in Swahili, and Captain Biggar limped up, rubbing his shin.

Mrs. Spottsworth was all womanly sympathy.

"Oh, dear. Have you hurt yourself, Captain?"

"A mere scratch, dear lady," he assured her.

He spoke bluffly, and only somebody like Sherlock Holmes or Monsieur Poirot could have divined that at the sound of her voice his soul had turned a double somersault leaving him quivering with an almost Bill Rowcester-like intensity.

His telephone conversation concluded, the White Hunter had prudently decided to avoid the living-room and head straight for the great open spaces, where he could be alone. To join the ladies, he had reasoned, would be to subject himself to the searing torture of having to sit and gaze at the woman he worshipped, a process which would simply rub in the fact of how unattainable she was. He recognized himself as being in the unfortunate position of the moth in Shelley's well-known poem that allowed itself to become attracted by a star, and it seemed to him that the smartest move a level-headed moth could make would be to minimize the anguish by shunning the adored object's society. It was, he felt, what Shelley would have advised.

And here he was, alone with her in the night, a night complete with moonlight, nightingales, gentle breezes and the scent of stock and tobacco plant.

It was a taut, tense Captain Biggar, a Captain Biggar telling himself he must be strong, who accepted his companion's invitation to join her on the rustic seat. The voices of Tubby Frobisher and the Subahdar seemed to ring in his ears. 'Chin up, old boy,' said

Tubby in his right ear. 'Remember the code,' said the Subahdar in his left.

He braced himself for the coming *tête-à-tête*.

Mrs. Spottsworth, a capital conversationalist, began it by saying what a beautiful night it was, to which the Captain replied "Top hole". "The moon", said Mrs. Spottsworth, indicating it and adding that she always thought a night when there was a full moon was so much nicer than a night when there was not a full moon. "Oh, rather," said the Captain. Then, after Mrs. Spottsworth had speculated as to whether the breeze was murmuring lullabies to the sleeping flowers and the Captain had regretted his inability to inform her on this point, he being a stranger in these parts, there was a silence.

It was broken by Mrs. Spottsworth, who gave a little cry of concern. "Oh, dear!"

"What's the matter?"

"I've dropped my pendant. The clasp is so loose."

Captain Biggar appreciated her emotion.

"Bad show," he agreed. "It must be on the ground somewhere. I'll have a look-see."

"I wish you would. It's not valuable—I don't suppose it cost more than ten thousand dollars—but it has a sentimental interest. One of my husbands gave it to me, I never can remember which. Oh, have you found it? Thank you ever so much. Will you put it on for me?"

As Captain Biggar did so, his fingers, spine and stomach muscles trembled. It is almost impossible to clasp a pendant round its owner's neck without touching that neck in spots, and he touched his companion's in several. And every time he touched it, something seemed to go through him like a knife. It was as though the moon, the nightingale, the breeze, the stock and the tobacco plant were calling to him to cover this neck with burning kisses.

Only Tubby Frobisher and the Subahdar, forming a solid *bloc* in opposition, restrained him.

'Straight bat, old boy!' said Tubby Frobisher.

'Remember you're a white man,' said the Subahdar.

He clenched his fists and was himself again.

"It must be jolly," he said, recovering his bluffness, "to be rich enough to think ten thousand dollars isn't anything to write home about."

Mrs. Spottsworth felt like an actor receiving a cue.

"Do you think that rich women are happy, Captain Biggar?"

The Captain said that all those he had met—and in his capacity of White Hunter he had met quite a number—had seemed pretty bobbish.

"They wore the mask."

"Eh?"

"They smiled to hide the ache in their hearts," explained Mrs. Spottsworth.

The Captain said he remembered one of them, a large blonde of the name of Fish, dancing the can-can one night in her step-ins, and Mrs. Spottsworth said that no doubt she was just trying to show a brave front to the world.

"Rich women are so lonely, Captain Biggar."

"Are *you* lonely?"

"Very, very lonely."

"Oh, ah," said the Captain.

It was not what he would have wished to say. He would have preferred to pour out his soul in a torrent of impassioned words. But what could a fellow do, with Tubby Frobisher and the Subahdar watching his every move?

A woman who has told a man in the moonlight, with nightingales singing their heads off in the background, that she is very, very lonely and received in response the words 'Oh, ah' is scarcely to be blamed for feeling a momentary pang of discouragement. Mrs. Spottsworth had once owned a large hound dog of lethargic temperament who could be induced to go out for his nightly airing only by a succession of sharp kicks. She was beginning to feel now as she had felt when her foot thudded against this languorous animal's posterior. The same depressing sense of trying in vain to move an immovable mass. She loved the White Hunter. She admired him. But when you set out to kindle the spark of passion in him, you certainly had a job on your hands. In a moment of bitterness she told herself that she had known oysters on the half-shell with more of the divine fire in them.

However, she persevered.

"How strange our meeting again like this," she said softly.

"Very odd."

"We were a whole world apart, and we met in an English inn."

"Quite a coincidence."

"Not a coincidence. It was destined. Shall I tell you what brought you to that inn?"

"I wanted a spot of beer."

"Fate," said Mrs. Spottsworth. "Destiny. I beg your pardon?"

"I was only saying that, come right down to it, there's no beer like English beer."

"The same Fate, the same Destiny," continued Mrs. Spottsworth, who at another moment would have hotly contested this statement, for she thought English beer undrinkable, "that brought us together in Kenya. Do you remember the day we met in Kenya?"

Captain Biggar writhed. It was like asking Joan of Arc if she happened to recall the time she saw that heavenly vision of hers. 'How about it, boys?' he inquired silently, looking pleadingly from right to left. 'Couldn't you stretch a point?' But Tubby Frobisher and the Subahdar shook their heads.

'The code, old man,' said Tubby Frobisher.

'Play the game, old boy,' said the Subahdar.

"Do you?" asked Mrs. Spottsworth.

"Oh, rather," said Captain Biggar.

"I had the strangest feeling, when I saw you that day, that we had met before in some previous existence."

"A bit unlikely, what?"

Mrs. Spottsworth closed her eyes.

"I seemed to see us in some dim, prehistoric age. We were clad in skins. You hit me over the head with your club and dragged me by my hair to your cave."

"Oh, no, dash it, I wouldn't do a thing like that."

Mrs. Spottsworth opened her eyes, and enlarging them to their fullest extent allowed them to play on his like searchlights.

"You did it because you loved me," she said in a low, vibrant whisper. "And I——"

She broke off. Something tall and willowy had loomed up against the skyline, and a voice with perhaps just a quaver of nervousness in it was saying 'Hullo-ullo-ullo-ullo-ullo'.

"I've been looking for you everywhere, Rosie," said Bill. "When I found you weren't at the ruined chapel . . . Oh, hullo, Captain."

"Hullo," said Captain Biggar dully, and tottered off. Lost in the shadows a few paces down the path, he halted and brushed away the beads of perspiration which had formed on his forehead.

He was breathing heavily, like a buffalo in the mating season. It had been a near thing, a very near thing. Had this interruption been postponed even for another minute, he knew that he must have sinned against the code and taken the irrevocable step which would have made his name a mockery and a byword in the Anglo-Malay Club at Kuala Lumpur. A pauper with a bank balance of a few meagre pounds, he would have been proposing marriage to a woman with millions.

More and more, as the moments went by, he had found himself being swept off his feet, his ears becoming deafer and deafer to the muttered warnings of Tubby Frobisher and the Subahdar. Her eyes he might have resisted. Her voice, too, and the skin he had loved to touch. But when it came to eyes, voice, skin, moonlight, gentle breezes from the west and nightingales, the mixture was too rich.

Yes, he felt as he stood there heaving like a stage sea, he had been saved, and it might have been supposed that his prevailing emotion would have been a prayerful gratitude to Fate or Destiny for its prompt action. But, oddly enough, it was not. The first spasm of relief had died quickly away, to be succeeded by a rising sensation of nausea. And what caused this nausea was the fact that, being still within earshot of the rustic seat, he could hear all that Bill was saying. And Bill, having seated himself beside Mrs. Spottsworth, had begun to coo.

Too little has been said in this chronicle of the ninth Earl of Rowcester's abilities in this direction. When we heard him promising his sister Monica to contact Mrs. Spottsworth and coo to her like a turtle dove, we probably formed in our minds the picture of one of those run-of-the-mill turtle doves whose cooing, though adequate, does not really amount to anything much. We would have done better to envisage something in the nature of a turtle dove of stellar quality, what might be called the Turtle Dove Supreme. A limited young man in many respects, Bill Rowcester could, when in mid-season form, touch heights in the way of cooing which left his audience, if at all impressionable, gasping for air.

These heights he was touching now, for the thought that this woman had it in her power to take England's leading white elephant off his hands, thus stabilizing his financial position and enabling him to liquidate Honest Patch Perkins' honourable obligations, lent him an eloquence which he had not achieved since May Week dances at Cambridge. The golden words came trickling from his lips like syrup.

Captain Biggar was not fond of syrup, and he did not like the thought of the woman he loved being subjected to all this goo. For a moment he toyed with the idea of striding up and breaking Bill's spine in three places, but once more found his aspirations blocked by the code. He had eaten Bill's meat and drunk Bill's drink . . . both excellent, especially the roast duck . . . and that made the feller immune to assault. For when a feller has accepted a feller's hospitality, a feller can't go about breaking the feller's spine, no matter what the feller may have done. The code is rigid on that point.

He is at liberty, however, to docket the feller in his mind as a low-down, fortune-hunting son of a what not, and this was how Captain Biggar was docketing Bill as he lumbered back to the house. And it was—substantially—how he described him to Jill when, passing through the French window, he found her crossing the living-room on her way to deposit her things in her sleeping apartment.

"Good gracious!" said Jill, intrigued by his aspect. "You seem very upset, Captain Biggar. What's the matter? Have you been bitten by an alligator?"

Before proceeding, the Captain had to put her straight on this.

"No alligators in England," he said. "Except, of course, in zoos. No, I have been shocked to the very depths of my soul."

"By a wombat?"

Again the Captain was obliged to correct her misapprehensions. An oddly ignorant girl, this, he was thinking.

"No wombats in England, either. What shocked me to the very depths of my soul was listening to a low-down, fortune-hunting English peer doing his stuff," he barked bitterly. "Lord Rowcester, he calls himself. Lord Gigolo's what I call him."

Jill started so sharply that she dropped her suitcase.

"Allow me," said the Captain, diving for it.

"I don't understand," said Jill. "Do you mean that Lord Rowcester——?"

One of the rules of the code is that a white man must shield women, and especially young, innocent girls, from the seamy side of life, but Captain Biggar was far too stirred to think of that now. He resembled Othello not only in his taste for antres vast and deserts idle but in his tendency, being wrought, to become perplexed in the extreme.

"He was making love to Mrs. Spottsworth in the moonlight," he said curtly.

"What!"

"Heard him with my own ears. He was cooing to her like a turtle dove. After her money, of course. All the same, these effete aristocrats of the old country. Make a noise like a rich widow anywhere in England, and out come all the Dukes and Earls and Viscounts, howling like wolves. Rats, we'd call them in Kuala Lumpur. You should hear Tubby Frobisher talk about them at the club. I remember him saying one day to Doc and Squiffy—the Subahdar wasn't there, if I recollect rightly—gone up country, or something—'Doc', he said . . . "

It was probably going to be a most extraordinarily good story, but Captain Biggar did not continue it any further for he saw that his audience was walking out on him. Jill had turned abruptly, and was passing through the door. Her head, he noted, was bowed, and very properly, too, after a revelation like that. Any nice girl would have been knocked endways by such a stunning *exposé* of the moral weaknesses of the British aristocracy.

He sat down and picked up the evening paper, throwing it from him with a stifled cry as the words 'Whistler's Mother' leaped at him from the printed page. He did not want to be reminded of Whistler's Mother. He was brooding darkly on Honest Patch Perkins and wondering wistfully if Destiny (or Fate) would ever bring their paths together again, when Jeeves came floating in. Simultaneously, Rory entered from the library.

"Oh, Jeeves," said Rory, "will you bring me a flagon of strong drink? I am athirst."

With a respectful movement of his head Jeeves indicated the tray he was carrying, laden with the right stuff, and Rory accompanied him to the table, licking his lips.

"Something for you, Captain?" he said.

"Whisky, if you please," said Captain Biggar. After that ordeal in the moonlit garden, he needed a restorative.

"Whisky? Right. And for you, Mrs. Spottsworth?" said Rory, as that lady came through the French window accompanied by Bill.

"Nothing, thank you, Sir Roderick. On a night like this, moonlight is enough for me. Moonlight and your lovely garden, Billiken."

"I'll tell you something about that garden," said Rory. "In the summer months——" He broke off as Monica appeared in the library door. The sight of her not only checked his observations on the garden, but reminded him of her injunction to boost the bally place to this Spottsworth woman. Looking about him for something in the bally place capable of being boosted, his eye fell on the dower chest in the corner and he recalled complimentary things he had heard said in the past about it.

It seemed to him that it would make a good *point d'appui*. "Yes," he proceeded, "the garden's terrific, and furthermore it must never be overlooked that Rowcester Abbey, though a bit shopsoiled and falling apart at the seams, contains many an *objet d'art* calculated to make the connoisseur sit up and say 'What ho!' Cast an eye on that dower chest, Mrs. Spottsworth."

"I was admiring it when I first arrived. It's beautiful."

"Yes, it is nice, isn't it?" said Monica, giving her husband a look of wifely approval. One didn't often find Rory showing such signs of almost human intelligence. "Duveen used to plead to be allowed to buy it, but of course it's an heirloom and can't be sold."

"Goes with the house," said Rory.

"It's full of the most wonderful old costumes."

"Which go with the house," said Rory, probably quite incorrectly, but showing zeal.

"Would you like to look at them?" said Monica, reaching for the lid.

Bill uttered an agonized cry.

"They're not in there!"

"Of course they are. They always have been. And I'm sure Rosalinda would enjoy seeing them."

"I would indeed."

"There's quite a romantic story attached to this dower chest, Rosalinda. The Lord Rowcester of that time—centuries ago— wouldn't let his daughter marry the man she loved, a famous explorer and discoverer."

"The old boy was against Discoverers," explained Rory. "He was afraid they might discover America. Ha, ha, ha, ha, ha. Oh, I beg your pardon."

"The lover sent his chest to the girl, filled with rare embroideries he had brought back from his travels in the East, and her father wouldn't let her have it. He told the lover to come and take it away. And the lover did, and of course inside it was the young man's bride. Knowing what was going to happen, she had hidden there."

"And the funny part of the story is that the old blister followed the chap all the way down the drive, shouting 'Get that damn thing out of here!' "

Mrs. Spottsworth was enchanted.

"What a delicious story. Do open it, Monica."

"I will. It isn't locked."

Bill sank bonelessly into a chair.

"Jeeves!"

"M'lord?"

"Brandy!"

"Very good, m'lord."

"Well, for heaven's sake!" said Monica.

She was staring wide-eyed at a check coat of loud pattern and a tie so crimson, so intensely blue horseshoed, that Rory shook his head censoriously.

"Good Lord, Bill, don't tell me you go around in a coat like that? It must make you look like an absconding bookie. And the tie! The cravat! Ye gods! You'd better drop in at Harrige's and see the chap in our haberdashery department. We've got a sale on."

Captain Biggar strode forward. There was a tense, hard expression on his rugged face.

"Let me look at that." He took the coat, felt in the pocket and produced a black patch. "Ha!" he said, and there was a wealth of meaning in his voice.

Rory was listening at the library door.

"Hullo," he said. "Someone talking French. Must be Boussac. Don't want to miss Boussac. Come along, Moke. This girl," said Rory, putting a loving arm round her shoulder, "talks French with both hands. You coming, Mrs. Spottsworth? It's the Derby Dinner on television."

"I will join you later, perhaps," said Mrs. Spottsworth. "I left Pomona out in the garden, and she may be getting lonely."

"You, Captain?"

Captain Biggar shook his head. His face was more rugged than ever.

"I have a word or two to say to Lord Rowcester first. If you can spare me a moment, Lord Rowcester?"

"Oh, rather," said Bill faintly.

Jeeves returned with the brandy, and he sprang for it like Whistler's Mother leaping at the winning post.

11

Bᴜᴛ brandy, when administered in one of those small after-dinner glasses, can never do anything really constructive for a man whose affairs have so shaped themselves as to give him the momentary illusion of having been hit in the small of the back by the Twentieth Century Limited. A tun or a hogshead of the stuff might have enabled Bill to face the coming interview with a jaunty smile. The mere sip which was all that had been vouchsafed to him left him as pallid and boneless as if it had been sarsaparilla. Gazing through a mist at Captain Biggar, he closely resembled the sort of man for whom the police spread drag-nets, preparatory to questioning them in connection with the recent smash-and-grab robbery at Marks and Schoenstein's Bon Ton Jewellery Store on Eighth Avenue. His face had shaded away to about the colour of the under-side of a dead fish, and Jeeves, eyeing him with respectful commiseration, wished that it were possible to bring the roses back to his cheeks by telling him one or two good things which had come into his mind from the *Collected Works of Marcus Aurelius*.

Captain Biggar, even when seen through a mist, presented a spectacle which might well have intimidated the stoutest. His eyes seemed to Bill to be shooting out long, curling flames, and why they called a man with a face as red as that a White Hunter was more than he was able to understand. Strong emotion, as always, had intensified the vermilion of the Captain's complexion, giving him something of the appearance of a survivor from an explosion in a tomato cannery.

Nor was his voice, when he spoke, of a timbre calculated to lull any apprehensions which his aspect might have inspired. It was the voice of a man who needed only a little sympathy and encouragement to make him whip out a revolver and start blazing away with it.

"So!" he said.

There are no good answers to the word 'So!' particularly when uttered in the kind of voice just described, and Bill did not attempt to find one.

"So you are Honest Patch Perkins!"

Jeeves intervened, doing his best as usual.

"Well, yes and no, sir."

"What do you mean, yes and no? Isn't this the louse's patch?" demanded the Captain, brandishing Exhibit A. "Isn't that the hellhound's ginger moustache?" he said, giving Exhibit B a twiddle. "And do you think I didn't recognize that coat and tie?"

"What I was endeavouring to convey by the expression 'Yes and no', sir, was that his lordship has retired from business."

"You bet he has. Pity he didn't do it sooner."

"Yes, sir. Oh, Iago, the pity of it, Iago."

"Eh?"

"I was quoting the Swan of Avon, sir."

"Well, stop quoting the bally Swan of Avon."

"Certainly, sir, if you wish it."

Bill had recovered his faculties to a certain extent. To say that even now he was feeling boomps-a-daisy would be an exaggeration, but he was capable of speech.

"Captain Biggar," he said, "I owe you an explanation."

"You owe me three thousand and five pounds two and six," said the Captain, coldly corrective.

This silenced Bill again, and the Captain took advantage of the fact to call him eleven derogatory names.

Jeeves assumed the burden of the defence, for Bill was still reeling under the impact of the eleventh name.

"It is impossible to gainsay the fact that in the circumstances your emotion is intelligible, sir, for one readily admits that his lordship's recent activities are of a nature to lend themselves to adverse criticism. But can one fairly blame his lordship for what has occurred?"

This seemed to the Captain an easy one to answer.

"Yes," he said.

"You will observe that I employed the adverb 'fairly', sir. His lordship arrived on Epsom Downs this afternoon with the best intentions and a capital adequate for any reasonable emergency. He could hardly have been expected to foresee that two such meagrely favoured animals as Lucy Glitters and Whistler's Mother would have emerged triumphant from their respective trials of speed. His lordship is not clairvoyant."

"He could have laid the bets off."

"There I am with you sir. *Rem acu tetigisti.*"

"Eh?"

"A Latin expression, which might be rendered in English by the American colloquialism 'You said a mouthful'. I urged his lordship to do so."

"You?"

"I was officiating as his lordship's clerk."

The Captain stared.

"You weren't the chap in the pink moustache?"

"Precisely, sir, though I would be inclined to describe it as russet rather than pink."

The Captain brightened.

"So you were his clerk, were you? Then when he goes to prison, you'll go with him."

"Let us hope there will be no such sad ending as that, sir."

"What do you mean, 'sad' ending?" said Captain Biggar.

There was an uncomfortable pause. The Captain broke it.

"Well, let's get down to it," he said. "No sense in wasting time. Properly speaking, I ought to charge this sheep-faced, shambling refugee from hell——"

"The name is Lord Rowcester, sir."

"No, it's not, it's Patch Perkins. Properly speaking, Perkins, you slinking reptile, I ought to charge you for petrol consumed on the journey here from Epsom, repairs to my car, which wouldn't have broken down if I hadn't had to push it so hard in the effort to catch you . . . and," he added, struck with an afterthought, "the two beers I had at the Goose and Gherkin while waiting for those repairs to be done. But I'm no hog. I'll settle for three thousand and five pounds two and six. Write me a cheque."

Bill passed a fevered hand through his hair.

"How can I write you a cheque?"

Captain Biggar clicked his tongue, impatient of this shilly-shallying.

"You have a pen, have you not? And there is ink on the premises, I imagine? You are a strong, able-bodied young fellow in full possession of the use of your right hand, aren't you? No paralysis? No rheumatism in the joints? If," he went on, making a concession, "what is bothering you is that you have run out of blotting paper, never mind. I'll blow on it."

Jeeves came to the rescue, helping out the young master, who was still massaging the top of his head.

"What his lordship is striving to express in words, sir, is that while, as you rightly say, he is physically competent to write a cheque for three thousand and five pounds two shillings and sixpence, such a cheque, when presented at your bank, would not be honoured."

"Exactly," said Bill, well pleased with this lucid way of putting the thing. "It would bounce like a bounding Dervish and come shooting back like a homing pigeon."

"Two very happy images, m'lord."

"I haven't a bean."

"Insufficient funds is the technical expression, m'lord. His lordship, if I may employ the argot, sir, is broke to the wide."

Captain Biggar stared.

"You mean you own a place like this, a bally palace if ever I saw one, and can't write a cheque for three thousand pounds?"

Jeeves undertook the burden of explanation.

"A house such as Rowcester Abbey, in these days is not an asset, sir, it is a liability. I fear that your long residence in the East has rendered you not quite abreast of the changed conditions prevailing in your native land. Socialistic legislation has sadly depleted the resources of England's hereditary aristocracy. We are living now in what is known as the Welfare State, which means—broadly—that everybody is completely destitute."

It would have seemed incredible to any of the native boys, hippopotami, rhinoceri, pumas, zebras, alligators and buffaloes with whom he had come in contact in the course of his long career in the wilds that Captain Biggar's strong jaw was capable of falling like an unsupported stick of asparagus, but it had fallen now in precisely that manner. There was something almost piteous in the way his blue eyes, round and dismayed, searched the faces of the two men before him.

"You mean he can't brass up?"

"You have put it in a nutshell, sir. Who steals his lordship's purse steals trash."

Captain Biggar, his iron self-control gone, became a human semaphore. He might have been a White Hunter doing his daily dozen.

"But I must have the money, and I must have it before noon tomorrow." His voice rose in what in a lesser man would have been a wail. "Listen. I'll have to let you in on something that's vitally secret, and if you breathe a word to a soul I'll rip you both asunder with my bare hands, shred you up into small pieces and jump on the remains with hobnailed boots. Is that understood?"

Bill considered.

"Yes, that seems pretty clear. Eh, Jeeves?"

"Most straightforward, m'lord."

"Carry on, Captain."

Captain Biggar lowered his voice to a rasping whisper.

"You remember that telephone call I made after dinner? It was to those pals of mine, the chaps who gave me my winning double this afternoon. Well, when I say winning double," said Captain Biggar, raising his voice a little, "that's what it would have been but for the degraded chiselling of a dastardly, lop-eared——"

"Quite, quite," said Bill hurriedly. "You telephoned to your friends, you were saying?"

"I was anxious to know if it was all settled."

"If all what was settled?"

Captain Biggar lowered his voice again, this time so far that his words sounded like gas escaping from a pipe.

"There's something cooking. As Shakespeare says, we have an enterprise of great importance."

Jeeves winced. " 'Enter*prises* of great pith and moment' is the exact quotation, sir."

"These chaps have a big S.P. job on for the Derby tomorrow. It's the biggest cert in the history of the race. The Irish horse, Ballymore."

Jeeves raised his eyebrows.

"Not generally fancied, sir."

"Well, Lucy Glitters and Whistler's Mother weren't generally fancied, were they? That's what makes this job so stupendous. Ballymore's a long-priced outsider. Nobody knows anything about him. He's been kept darker than a black cat on a moonless night. But let me tell you that he has had two secret trial gallops over the Epsom course and broke the record both times."

Despite his agitation, Bill whistled.

"You're sure of that?"

"Beyond all possibility of doubt. I've watched the animal run with my own eyes, and it's like a streak of lightning. All you see is a sort of brown blur. We're putting our money on at the last moment, carefully distributed among a dozen different bookies so as not to upset the price. And now," cried Captain Biggar, his voice rising once more, "you're telling me that I shan't have any money to put on."

His agony touched Bill. He did not think, from what little he had seen of him, that Captain Biggar was a man with whom he could ever form one of those beautiful friendships you read about, the kind that existed between Damon and Pythias, David and Jonathan, or Swan and Edgar, but he could understand and sympathize with his grief.

"Too bad, I agree," he said, giving the fermenting hunter a kindly, brotherly look and almost, but not quite, patting him on the shoulder. "The whole situation is most regrettable, and you wouldn't be far out in saying that the spectacle of your anguish gashes me like a knife. But I'm afraid the best I can manage is a series of monthly payments, starting say about six weeks from now."

"That's won't do me any good."

"Nor me," said Bill frankly. "It'll knock the stuffing out of my budget and mean cutting down the necessities of life to the barest minimum. I doubt if I shall be able to afford another square meal till about 1954. Farewell, a long farewell . . . to what, Jeeves?"

"To all your greatness, m'lord. This is the state of man: today he puts forth the tender leaves of hopes; tomorrow blossoms, and bears his blushing honours thick upon him. The third day comes a frost, a killing frost, and when he thinks, good easy man, full surely his greatness is a-ripening, nips his roots."

"Thank you, Jeeves."

"Not at all, m'lord."

Bill looked at him and sighed.

"You'll have to go, you know, to start with. I can't possibly pay your salary."

"I should be delighted to serve your lordship without emolument."

"That's dashed good of you, Jeeves, and I appreciate it. About as nifty a display of the feudal spirit as I ever struck. But how," asked Bill keenly, "could I keep you in fish?"

Captain Biggar interrupted these courteous exchanges. For some moments he had been chafing, if chafing is the right word to describe a White Hunter who is within an ace of frothing at the mouth. He said something so forceful about Jeeves's fish that speech was wiped from Bill's lips and he stood goggling with the dumb consternation of a man who has been unexpectedly struck by a thunderbolt.

"I've got to have that money!"

"His lordship has already informed you that, owing to the circumstance of his being fiscally crippled, that is impossible."

"Why can't he borrow it?"

Bill recovered the use of his vocal cords.

"Who from?" he demanded peevishly. "You talk as if borrowing money was as simple as falling off a log."

"The point his lordship is endeavouring to establish," explained Jeeves, "is the almost universal tendency of gentlemen to prove unco-operative when an attempt is made to float a loan at their expense."

"Especially if what you're trying to get into their ribs for is a whacking great sum like three thousand and five pounds two and six."

"Precisely, m'lord. Confronted by such figures, they become like the deaf adder that hearkens not to the voice of the charmer, charming never so wisely."

"So putting the bite on my social circle is off," said Bill. "It can't be done. I'm sorry."

Captain Biggar seemed to blow flame through his nostrils.

"You'll be sorrier," he said, "and I'll tell you when. When you and this precious clerk of yours are standing in the dock at the Old Bailey, with the Judge looking at you over his bifocals and me in the well of the court making faces at you. Then's the time when you'll be sorry . . . then and shortly afterwards, when the Judge pronounces sentence, accompanied by some strong remarks from the bench, and they lead you off to Wormwood Scrubs to start doing your two years hard or whatever it is."

Bill gaped.

"Oh, dash it!" he protested. "You wouldn't proceed to that . . . what, Jeeves?"

"Awful extreme, m'lord.'

"You surely wouldn't proceed to that awful extreme?"

"Wouldn't I!"

"One doesn't want unpleasantness."

"What one wants and what one is going to get are two different things," said Captain Biggar, and went out, grinding his teeth, to cool off in the garden.

He left behind him one of those silences often called pregnant. Bill was the first to speak.

"We're in the soup, Jeeves."

"Certainly a somewhat sharp crisis in our affairs would appear to have been precipitated, m'lord."

"He wants his pound of flesh."

"Yes, m'lord."

"And we haven't any flesh."

"No, m'lord. It is a most disagreeable state of affairs."

"He's a tough egg, that Biggar. He looks like a gorilla with stomach-ache."

"There is, perhaps, a resemblance to such an animal, afflicted as your lordship suggests."

"Did you notice him at dinner?"

"To which aspect of his demeanour during the meal does your lordship allude?"

"I was thinking of the sinister way he tucked into the roast duck. He flung himself on it like a tiger on its prey. He gave me the impression of a man without ruth or pity."

"Unquestionably a gentleman lacking in the softer emotions, m'lord."

"There's a word that just describes him. Begins with a V. Not vapid. Not vermicelli. Vindictive. The chap's vindictive. I can understand him being sore about not getting his money, but what good will it do him to ruin me?"

"No doubt he will derive a certain moody satisfaction from it, m'lord."

Bill brooded.

"I suppose there really is nobody one could borrow a bit of cash from?"

"Nobody who springs immediately to the mind, m'lord."

"How about that financier fellow, who lives out Ditchingham way—Sir Somebody Something?"

"Sir Oscar Wopple, m'lord? He shot himself last Friday."

"Oh, then we won't bother him."

Jeeves coughed.

"If I might make a suggestion, m'lord?"

"Yes, Jeeves?"

A faint ray of hope had stolen into Bill's sombre eyes. His voice, while still scarcely to be described as animated, no longer resembled that of a corpse speaking from the tomb.

"It occurred to me as a passing thought, m'lord, that were we to possess ourselves of Captain Biggar's ticket, our position would be noticeably stabilized."

Bill shook his head.

"I don't get you, Jeeves. Ticket? What ticket? You speak as if this were a railway station."

"I refer to the ticket which, in my capacity of your lordship's clerk, I handed to the gentleman as a record of his wager on Lucy Glitters and Whistler's Mother, m'lord."

"Oh, you mean his *ticket*?" said Bill, enlightened.

"Precisely, m'lord. As he left the racecourse so abruptly, it must still be upon his person, and it is the only evidence that exists that the wager was ever made. Once we had deprived him of it, your lordship would be in a position to make payment at your lordship's leisure."

"I see. Yes, that would be nice. So we get the ticket from him, do we?"

"Yes, m'lord."

"May I say one word, Jeeves?"

"Certainly, m'lord."

"How?"

"By what I might describe as direct action, m'lord."

Bill stared. This opened up a new line of thought.

"Set on him, you mean? *Scrag* him? Choke it out of him?"

"Your lordship has interpreted my meaning exactly."

Bill continued to stare.

"But, Jeeves, have you *seen* him? That bulging chest, those rippling muscles?"

"I agree that Captain Biggar is well-nourished, m'lord, but we would have the advantage of surprise. The gentleman went out into the garden. When he returns, one may assume that it will be by way of the French window by which he made his egress. If I draw the curtains, it will be necessary for him to enter through them. We will see him fumbling, and in that moment a sharp tug will cause the curtains to descend upon him, enmeshing him, as it were."

Bill was impressed, as who would not have been.

"By Jove, Jeeves! Now you're talking. You think it would work?"

"Unquestionably, m'lord. The method is that of the Roman retiarius, with whose technique your lordship is no doubt familiar."

"That was the bird who fought with net and trident?"

"Precisely, m'lord. So if your lordship approves—"

"You bet I approve."

"Very good, m'lord. Then I will draw the curtains now, and we will take up our stations on either side of them."

It was with deep satisfaction that Bill surveyed the completed preparations. After a rocky start, the sun was coming through the cloud wrack.

"It's in the bag, Jeeves!"

"A very apt image, m'lord."

"If he yells, we will stifle his cries with the . . . what do you call this stuff"

"Velours, m'lord."

"We will stifle his cries with the velours. And while he's grovelling on the ground, I shall get a chance to give him a good kick in the tailpiece."

"There *is* that added attraction, m'lord. For blessings ever wait on virtuous deeds, as the playwright Congreve informs us."

Bill breathed heavily.

"Were you in the first world war, Jeeves?"

"I dabbled in it to a certain extent, m'lord."

"I missed that one because I wasn't born, but I was in the Commandos in this last one. This is rather like waiting for zero hour, isn't it?"

"The sensation is not dissimilar, m'lord."

"He should be coming soon."

"Yes, m'lord."

"On your toes, Jeeves!"

"Yes, m'lord."

"All set?"

"Yes, m'lord."

"Hi!" said Captain Biggar in their immediate rear. "I want to have another word with you two."

A lifetime of braving the snares and perils of the wilds develops in those White Hunters over the years a sort of sixth sense, warning them of lurking danger. Where the ordinary man, happening upon a tiger trap in the jungle, would fall in base over apex, your White Hunter, saved by his sixth sense, walks round it.

With fiendish cunning, Captain Biggar, instead of entering, as expected, through the French window, had circled the house and come in by the front door.

⋆ 12 ⋆

ALTHOUGH the actual time which had elapsed between Captain Biggar's departure and return had been only about five minutes, scarcely long enough for him to take half a dozen turns up and down the lawn, pausing in the course of one of them to kick petulantly at a passing frog, it had been ample for his purposes. If you had said to him as he was going through the French window 'Have you any ideas, Captain?' he would have been forced to reply 'No more than a rabbit'. But now his eye was bright and his manner jaunty. He had seen the way.

On occasions of intense spiritual turmoil the brain works quickly. Thwarted passion stimulates the little grey cells, and that painful scene on the rustic seat, when love had collided so disastrously with the code that governs the actions of the men who live on the frontiers of Empire, had stirred up those of Captain Biggar till, if you had X-rayed his skull, you would have seen them leaping and dancing like rice in a saucepan. Not thirty seconds after the frog, rubbing its head, had gone off to warn the other frogs to watch out for atom bombs, he was rewarded with what he recognized immediately as an inspiration.

Here was his position in a nutshell. He loved. Right. He would go further, he loved like the dickens. And unless he had placed a totally wrong construction on her words, her manner and the light in her eyes, the object of his passion loved him. A woman, he meant to say, does not go out of her way to bring the conversation round to the dear old days when a feller used to whack her over the top-knot with clubs and drag her into caves, unless she intends to convey a certain impression. True, a couple of minutes later she had been laughing and giggling with the frightful Rowcester excrescence, but that, it seemed to him now that he had had time to simmer down, had been merely a guest's conventional civility to a host. He dismissed the Rowcester gumboil as negligible. He was convinced that, if one went by the form book, he had but to lay his heart at her feet, and she would pick it up.

So far, so good. But here the thing began to get more complicated. She was rich and he was poor. That was the hitch. That was the snag. That was what was putting the good old sand in the bally machinery.

The thought that seared his soul and lent additional vigour to the kick he had directed at the frog was that, but for the deplorable financial methods of that black-hearted bookmaker, Honest Patch Rowcester, it would all have been so simple. Three thousand pounds deposited on the nose of Ballymore at the current odds of fifty to one would have meant a return of a hundred and fifty thousand, just like finding it: and surely even Tubby Frobisher and the Subahdar, rigid though their views were, could scarcely accuse a chap of not playing with the straight bat if he married a woman, however wealthy, while himself in possession of a hundred and fifty thousand of the best and brightest.

He groaned in spirit. A sorrow's crown of sorrow is remembering happier things, and he proceeded to torture himself with the recollection of how her neck had felt beneath his fingers as he fastened her pen——

Captain Biggar uttered a short, sharp exclamation. It was in Swahili, a language which always came most readily to his lips in moments of emotion, but its meaning was as clear as if it had been the 'Eureka!' of Archimedes.

Her pendant! Yes, now he saw daylight. Now he could start handling the situation as it should be handled.

Two minutes later, he was at the front door. Two minutes and twenty-five seconds later, he was in the living-room, eyeing the backs of Honest Patch Rowcester and his clerk as they stood—for some silly reason known only to themselves—crouching beside the curtains which they had pulled across the French window.

"Hi!" he cried. "I want to have another word with you two."

The effect of the observation on his audience was immediate and impressive. It is always disconcerting, when you are expecting a man from the north-east, to have him suddenly bark at you from the south-west, especially if he does so in a manner that recalls feeding-time in a dog hospital, and Bill went into his quaking and leaping routine with the smoothness that comes from steady practice. Even Jeeves, though his features did not lose their customary impassivity, appeared—if one could judge by the fact that his left eyebrow flickered for a moment as if about to rise—to have been stirred to quite a considerable extent.

"And don't stand there looking like a dying duck," said the Captain, addressing Bill, who, one is compelled to admit, was giving a rather close impersonation of such a bird *in articulo mortis*. "Since I saw you two beauties last," he continued, helping himself to another whisky and soda, "I have been thinking over the situation, and I have now got it all taped out. It suddenly came to me, quick as a flash. I said to myself 'The pendant!' "

Bill blinked feebly. His heart, which had crashed against the back of his front teeth, was slowly returning to its base, but it seemed to him that the shock which he had just sustained must have left his hearing impaired. It had sounded exactly as if the Captain had said 'The pendant!' which, of course, made no sense whatever.

"The pendant?" he echoed, groping.

"Mrs. Spottsworth is wearing a diamond pendant, m'lord," said Jeeves. "It is to this, no doubt, that the gentleman alludes."

It was specious, but Bill found himself still far from convinced. "You think so?"

"Yes, m'lord."

"He alludes to that, in your opinion?"

"Yes, m'lord."

"But why does he allude to it, Jeeves?"

"That, one is disposed to imagine, m'lord, one will ascertain when the gentleman has resumed his remarks."

"Gone on speaking, you mean?"

"Precisely, m'lord."

"Well, if you say so," said Bill doubtfully. "But it seems a . . . what's the expression you're always using?"

"Remote contingency, m'lord?"

"That's right. It seems a very remote contingency."

Captain Biggar had been fuming silently. He now spoke with not a little asperity.

"If you have quite finished babbling, Patch Rowcester——"

"Was I babbling?"

"Certainly you were babbling. You were babbling like a . . . like a . . . well, like whatever the dashed things are that babble."

"Brooks," said Jeeves helpfully, "are sometimes described as doing so, sir. In his widely-read poem of that name, the late Lord Tennyson puts the words 'Oh, brook, oh, babbling brook' into the mouth of the character Edmund, and later describes the rivulet, speaking in its own person, as observing 'I chatter over stony ways in little sharps and trebles, I bubble into eddying bays, I babble on the pebbles'."

Captain Biggar frowned.

"*Ai deng hahp kamoo* for the late Lord Tennyson," he said impatiently. "What I'm interested in is this pendant."

Bill looked at him with a touch of hope.

"Are you going to explain about that pendant? Throw light upon it, as it were?"

"I am. It's worth close on three thousand quid, and," said Captain Biggar, throwing out the observation almost casually, "you're going to pinch it, Patch Rowcester."

Bill gaped.

"Pinch it?"

"This very night."

It is always difficult for a man who is feeling as if he has just been struck over the occiput by a blunt instrument to draw himself to his full height and stare at someone censoriously, but Bill contrived to do so.

"What!" he cried, shocked to the core. "Are you, a bulwark of the Empire, a man who goes about setting an example to Dyaks, seriously suggesting that I rob one of my guests?"

"Well, I'm one of your guests, and you robbed me."

"Only temporarily."

"And you'll be robbing Mrs. Spottsworth only temporarily. I shouldn't have used the word 'pinch'. All I want you to do is borrow that pendant till tomorrow afternoon, when it will be returned."

Bill clutched his hair.

"Jeeves!"

"M'lord?"

"Rally round, Jeeves. My brain's tottering. Can you make any sense of what this rhinoceros-biffer is saying?"

"Yes, m'lord."

"You can? Then you're a better man than I am, Gunga Din."

"Captain Biggar's thought-processes seem to me reasonably clear, m'lord. The gentleman is urgently in need of money with which to back the horse Ballymore in tomorrow's Derby, and his proposal, as I take it, is that the pendant shall be abstracted and pawned and the proceeds employed for that purpose. Have I outlined your suggestion correctly, sir?"

"You have."

"At the conclusion of the race, one presumes, the object in question would be redeemed, brought back to the house, discovered, possibly by myself, in some spot where the lady might be supposed to have dropped it, and duly returned to her. Do I err in advancing this theory, sir?"

"You do not."

"Then, could one be certain beyond the peradventure of a doubt that Ballymore will win——"

"He'll win all right. I told you he had twice broken the course record."

"That is official, sir?"

"Straight from the feed-box."

"Then I must confess, m'lord, I see little or no objection to the scheme."

Bill shook his head, unconvinced.

"I still call it stealing."

Captain Biggar clicked his tongue.

"It isn't anything of the sort, and I'll tell you why. In a way, you might say that that pendant was really mine."

"Really . . . what was that last word?"

"Mine. Let me," said Captain Biggar, "tell you a little story."

He sat musing for a while. Coming out of his reverie and discovering with a start that his glass was empty, he refilled it. His attitude was that of a man, who, even if nothing came of the business transaction which he had proposed, intended to save something from the wreck by drinking as much as possible of his host's whisky. When the refreshing draught had finished its journey down the hatch, he wiped his lips on the back of his hand, and began.

"Do either of you chaps know the Long Bar at Shanghai? No? Well, it's the Café de la Paix of the East. They always say that if you sit outside the Café de la Paix in Paris long enough, you're sure sooner or later to meet all your pals, and it's the same with the Long Bar. A few years ago, chancing to be in Shanghai, I had dropped in there, never dreaming that Tubby Frobisher and the Subahdar were within a thousand miles of the place, and I'm dashed if the first thing I saw wasn't the two old bounders sitting on a couple of stools as large as life. 'Hullo, there, Bwana, old boy,' they said when I rolled up, and I said, 'Hullo, there, Tubby! Hullo there, Subahdar, old chap,' and Tubby said 'What'll you have, old boy?' and I said 'What are you boys having?' and they said stingahs, so I said that would do me all right, so Tubby ordered a round of stingahs, and we started talking about *chow-*

luangs and *nai bahn rot fais* and where we had all met last and
whatever became of the *poogni* at Lampang and all that sort of
thing. And when the stingahs were finished, I said 'The next are
on me. What for you, Tubby, old boy?' and he said he'd stick to
stingahs. 'And for you, Subahdar, old boy?' I said, and the
Subahdar said he'd stick to stingahs, too, so I wig-wagged the
barman and ordered stingahs all round, and, to cut a long story
short, the stingahs came, a stingah for Tubby, a stingah for the
Subahdar, and a stingah for me. 'Luck, old boys!' said Tubby.
'Luck, old boys!' said the Subahdar. 'Cheerio, old boys!' I said,
and we drank the stingahs."

Jeeves coughed. It was a respectful cough, but firm.

"Excuse me, sir."

"Eh?"

"I am reluctant to interrupt the flow of your narrative, but is
this leading somewhere?"

Captain Biggar flushed. A man who is telling a crisp, well-knit
story does not like to be asked if it is leading somewhere.

"Leading somewhere? What do you mean, is it leading somewhere? Of course it's leading somewhere. I'm coming to the nub
of the thing now. Scarcely had we finished this second round of
stingahs, when in through the door, sneaking along like a chap
that expects at any moment to be slung out on his fanny, came this
fellow in the tattered shirt and dungarees."

The introduction of a new and unexpected character took Bill
by surprise.

"Which fellow in the tattered shirt and dungarees?"

"This fellow I'm telling you about."

"Who was he?"

"You may well ask. Didn't know him from Adam, and I could
see Tubby Frobisher didn't know him from Adam. Nor did the
Subahdar. But he came sidling up to us and the first thing he said,
addressing me, was 'Hullo, Bimbo, old boy', and I stared and said
'Who on earth are you, old boy?' because I hadn't been called
Bimbo since I left school. Everybody called me that there, God
knows why, but out East it's been 'Bwana' for as long as I can
remember. And he said 'Don't you know me, old boy? I'm Sycamore, old boy'. And I stared again, and I said 'What's that, old
boy? Sycamore? Sycamore? Not Beau Sycamore that was in the
Army Class at Uppingham with me, old boy?' and he said 'That's
right, old boy. Only it's Hobo Sycamore now'."

The memory of that distressing encounter unmanned Captain Biggar for a moment. He was obliged to refill his glass with Bill's whisky before he could proceed.

"You could have knocked me down with a feather," he said, resuming. "This chap Sycamore had been the smartest, most dapper chap that ever adorned an Army Class, even at Uppingham."

Bill was following the narrative closely now.

"They're dapper in the Army Class at Uppingham, are they?"

"Very dapper, and this chap Sycamore, as I say, the most dapper of the lot. His dapperness was a byword. And here he was in a tattered shirt and dungarees, not even wearing a school tie." Captain Biggar sighed. "I saw at once what must have happened. It was the old, old story. Morale can crumble very easily out East. Drink, women and unpaid gambling debts . . ."

"Yes, yes," said Bill. "He'd gone under, had he?"

"Right under. It was pitiful. The chap was nothing but a bally beachcomber."

"I remember a story of Maugham's about a fellow like that."

"I'll bet your friend Maugham, whoever he may be, never met such a derelict as Sycamore. He had touched bottom, and the problem was what was to be done about it. Tubby Frobisher and the Subahdar, of course, not having been introduced, were looking the other way and taking no part in the conversation, so it was up to me. Well, there isn't much you can do for these chaps who have let the East crumble their morale except give them something to buy a couple of drinks with, and I was just starting to feel in my pocket for a *baht* or a *tical*, when from under that tattered shirt of his this chap Sycamore produced something that brought a gasp to my lips. Even Tubby Frobisher and the Subahdar, though they hadn't been introduced, had to stop trying to pretend there wasn't anybody there and sit up and take notice. '*Sabaiga!*' said Tubby. '*Pom bahoo!*' said the Subahdar. And I don't wonder they were surprised. It was this pendant which you have seen tonight on the neck . . ." Captain Biggar faltered for a moment. He was remembering how that neck had felt beneath his fingers. ". . . on the neck," he proceeded, calling all his manhood to his aid, "of Mrs. Spottsworth."

"Golly!" said Bill, and even Jeeves, from the fact that the muscle at the side of his mouth twitched briefly, seemed to be feeling that after a slow start the story had begun to move. One saw now that all that stingah stuff had been merely the artful establishing of atmosphere, the setting of the stage for the big scene.

" 'I suppose you wouldn't care to buy this, Bimbo, old boy?' this chap Sycamore said, waggling the thing to make it glitter. And I said 'Fry me in olive oil, Beau, old boy, where did you get that?'."

"That's just what I was going to ask," said Bill, all agog. "Where did he?"

"God knows. I ought not to have inquired. It was dashed bad form. That's one thing you learn very early out East of Suez. Never ask questions. No doubt there was some dark history behind the thing . . . robbery . . . possibly murder. I didn't ask. All I said was 'How much?' and he named a price far beyond the resources of my purse, and it looked as though the thing was going to be a washout. But fortunately Tubby Frobisher and the Subahdar—I'd introduced them by this time—offered to chip in, and between us we met his figure and he went off, back into the murk and shadows from which he had emerged. Sad thing, very sad. I remember seeing this chap Sycamore make a hundred and forty-six in a house cricket match at school before being caught low down in the gully off a googly that dipped and swung away late. On a sticky wicket, too," said Captain Biggar, and was silent for awhile, his thoughts in the past.

He came back into the present.

"So there you are," he said, with the air of one who has told a well-rounded tale.

"But how did you get it?" said Bill.

"Eh?"

"The pendant. You said it was yours, and the way I see it is that it passed into the possession of a syndicate."

"Oh, ah, yes, I didn't tell you that, did I? We shook dice for it and I won. Tubby was never lucky with the bones. Nor was the Subahdar."

"And how did Mrs. Spottsworth get it?"

"I gave it her."

"You *gave* it her?"

"Why not? The dashed thing was no use to me, and I had received many kindnesses from Mrs. Spottsworth and her husband. Poor chap was killed by a lion and what was left of him shipped off to Nairobi, and when Mrs. Spottsworth was leaving the camp on the following day I thought it would be a civil thing to give her something as a memento and all that, so I lugged out the pendant and asked her if she'd care to have it. She said she would, so I slipped it to her, and she went off with it. That's what I meant when I said you might say that the bally thing was really mine," said Captain Biggar, and helped himself to another whisky.

Bill was impressed.

"This puts a different complexion on things, Jeeves."

"Distinctly, m'lord."

"After all, as Pop Biggar says, the pendant practically belongs to him, and he merely wants to borrow it for an hour or two."

"Precisely, m'lord."

Bill turned to the Captain. His mind was made up.

"It's a deal," he said.

"You'll do it?"

"I'll have a shot."

"Stout fellow!"

"Let's hope it comes off."

"It'll come off all right. The clasp is loose."

"I meant I hoped nothing would go wrong."

Captain Biggar scouted the idea. He was all buoyancy and optimism.

"Go wrong? What can possibly go wrong? You'll be able to think of a hundred ways of getting the dashed thing, two brainy fellers like you. Well," said the Captain, finishing his whisky, "I'll be going out and doing my exercises."

"At this time of night?"

"Breathing exercises," explained Captain Biggar. "Yoga. And with it, of course, communion with the Jivatma or soul. Toodle-oo, chaps."

He pushed the curtains aside, and passed through the French window.

13

A LONG and thoughtful silence followed his departure. The room seemed very still, as rooms always did when Captain Biggar went out of them. Bill was sitting with his chin supported by his hand, like Rodin's Penseur. Then he looked at Jeeves and, having looked, shook his head.

"No, Jeeves," he said.

"M'lord?"

"I can see that feudal gleam in your eye, Jeeves. You are straining at the leash, all eagerness to lend the young master a helping hand. Am I right?"

"I was certainly feeling, m'lord, that in view of our relationship of thane and vassal it was my duty to afford your lordship all the assistance that lay within my power."

Bill shook his head again.

"No, Jeeves, that's out. Nothing will induce me to allow you to go getting yourself mixed up in an enterprise which, should things not pan out as planned, may quite possibly culminate in a five-year stretch at one of our popular prisons. I shall handle this binge alone, and I want no back-chat about it."

"But, m'lord——"

"No back-chat, I said, Jeeves."

"Very good, m'lord."

"All I require from you is advice and counsel. Let us review the position of affairs. We have here a diamond pendant which at the moment of going to press is on the person of Mrs. Spottsworth. The task confronting me—I said me, Jeeves—is somehow to detach this pendant from this person and nip away with it unobserved. Any suggestions?"

"The problem is undoubtedly one that presents certain points of interest, m'lord."

"Yes, I'd got as far as that myself."

"One rules out anything in the nature of violence, I presume, placing reliance wholly on stealth and finesse."

"One certainly does. Dismiss any idea that I propose to swat Mrs. Spottsworth on the napper with a blackjack."

"Then I would be inclined to say, m'lord, that the best results would probably be obtained from what I might term the spider sequence."

"I don't get you, Jeeves."

"If I might explain, m'lord. Your lordship will be joining the lady in the garden?"

"Probably on a rustic seat."

"Then, as I see it, m'lord, conditions will be admirably adapted to the plan I advocate. If shortly after entering into conversation with Mrs. Spottsworth, your lordship were to affect to observe a spider on her hair, the spider sequence would follow as doth the night the day. It would be natural for your lordship to offer to brush the insect off. This would enable your lordship to operate with your lordship's fingers in the neighbourhood of the lady's neck. And if the clasp, as Captain Biggar assures us, is loose, it will be a simple matter to unfasten the pendant and cause it to fall to the ground. Do I make myself clear, m'lord?"

"All straight so far. But wouldn't she pick it up?"

"No, m'lord, because in actual fact it would be in your lordship's pocket. Your lordship would institute a search in the surrounding grass, but without avail, and eventually the search would be abandoned until the following day. The object would finally be discovered late tomorrow evening."

"After Biggar gets back?"

"Precisely, m'lord."

"Nestling under a bush?"

"Or on the turf some little distance away. It had rolled."

"Do pendants roll?"

"This pendant would have done so, m'lord."

Bill chewed his lower lip thoughtfully.

"So that's the spider sequence?"

"That is the spider sequence, m'lord."

"Not a bad scheme at all."

"It has the merit of simplicity, m'lord. And if your lordship is experiencing any uneasiness at the thought of opening cold, as the theatrical expression is, I would suggest our having what in stage parlance is called a quick run through."

"A rehearsal, you mean?"

"Precisely, m'lord. It would enable your lordship to perfect yourself in lines and business. In the Broadway section of New York, where the theatre industry of the United States of America is centred, I am told that this is known as ironing out the bugs."

"Ironing out the spiders."

"Ha, ha, m'lord. But, if I may venture to say so, it is unwise to waste the precious moments in verbal pleasantries."

"Time is of the essence?"

"Precisely, m'lord. Would your lordship like to walk the scene?"

"Yes, I think I would, if you say it's going to steady the nervous system. I feel as if a troupe of performing fleas were practising buck-and-wing steps up and down my spine."

"I have heard Mr. Wooster complain of a similar malaise in moments of stress and trial, m'lord. It will pass."

"When?"

"As soon as your lordship has got the feel of the part. A rustic seat, your lordship said?"

"That's where she was last time."

"Scene, A rustic seat," murmured Jeeves. "Time, A night in summer. Discovered at rise, Mrs. Spottsworth. Enter Lord Rowcester. I will portray Mrs. Spottsworth, m'lord. We open with a few lines of dialogue to establish atmosphere, then bridge into the spider sequence. Your lordship speaks."

Bill marshalled his thoughts.

"Er—Tell me, Rosie——"

"Rosie, m'lord?"

"Yes, Rosie, blast it. Any objection?"

"None whatever, m'lord."

"I used to know her at Cannes."

"Indeed, m'lord? I was not aware. You were saying, m'lord?"

"Tell me, Rosie, are you afraid of spiders?"

"Why does your lordship ask?"

"There's rather an outsize specimen crawling on the back of your hair." Bill sprang about six inches in the direction of the ceiling. "What on earth did you do that for?" he demanded irritably.

Jeeves preserved his calm.

"My reason for screaming, m'lord, was merely to add verisimilitude. I supposed that that was how a delicately nurtured lady would be inclined to react on receipt of such a piece of information."

"Well, I wish you hadn't. The top of my head nearly came off."

"I am sorry, m'lord. But it was how I saw the scene. I felt it, felt it *here*," said Jeeves, tapping the left side of his waistcoat. "If your lordship would be good enough to throw me the line once more."

"There's rather an outsize specimen crawling on the back of your hair."

"I would be grateful if your lordship would be so kind as to knock it off."

"I can't see it now. Ah, there it goes. On your neck."

"And that," said Jeeves, rising from the settee on which in his role of Mrs. Spottsworth he had seated himself, "is cue for business, m'lord. Your lordship will admit that it is really quite simple."

"I suppose it is."

"I am sure that after this try-out the performing fleas to which your lordship alluded a moment ago will have substantially modified their activities."

"They've slowed up a bit, yes. But I'm still nervous."

"Inevitable on the eve of an opening performance, m'lord. I think your lordship should be starting as soon as possible. If 'twere done, then 'twere well 'twere done quickly. Our arrangements have been made with a view to a garden set, and it would be disconcerting were Mrs. Spottsworth to return to the house, compelling your lordship to adapt your technique to an interior."

Bill nodded.

"I see what you mean. Right ho, Jeeves. Good-bye."

"Good-bye, m'lord."

"If anything goes wrong——"

"Nothing will go wrong, m'lord."

"But if it does . . . You'll write to me in Dartmoor occasionally, Jeeves? Just a chatty letter from time to time, giving me the latest news from the outer world?"

"Certainly, m'lord."

"It'll cheer me up as I crack my daily rock. They tell me conditions are much better in these modern prisons than they used to be in the old days."

"So I understand, m'lord."

"I might find Dartmoor a regular home from home. Solid comfort, I mean to say."

"Quite conceivably, m'lord."

"Still, we'll hope it won't come to that."

"Yes, m'lord."

"Yes . . . Well, good-bye once again, Jeeves."

"Good-bye, m'lord."

Bill squared his shoulders and strode out, a gallant figure. He had summoned the pride of the Rowcesters to his aid, and it buoyed him up. With just this quiet courage had a Rowcester of the seventeenth century mounted the scaffold at Tower Hill, nodding affably to the headsman and waving to friends and relations in the audience. When the test comes, blood will tell.

He had been gone a few moments, when Jill came in.

It seemed to Jeeves that in the course of the past few hours the young master's betrothed had lost a good deal of the animation which rendered her as a rule so attractive, and he was right. Her recent interview with Captain Biggar had left Jill pensive and inclined to lower the corners of the mouth and stare mournfully. She was staring mournfully now.

"Have you seen Lord Rowcester, Jeeves?"

"His lordship has just stepped into the garden, miss."

"Where are the others?"

"Sir Roderick and her ladyship are still in the library, miss."

"And Mrs. Spottsworth?"

"She stepped into the garden shortly before his lordship."

Jill stiffened.

"Oh?" she said, and went into the library to join Monica and Rory. The corners of her mouth were drooping more than ever, and her stare had increased in mournfulness some twenty per cent. She looked like a girl who is thinking the worst, and that was precisely the sort of girl she was.

Two minutes later, Captain Biggar came bustling in with a song on his lips. Yoga and communion with the Jivatma or soul seemed to have done him good. His eyes were bright and his manner alert. It is when the time for action has come that you always catch these White Hunters at their best.

"Pale hands I loved beside the Shalimar, where are you now, where are you now?" sang Captain Biggar. "I . . . how does the dashed thing go . . . I sink beneath your spell. La, la, la . . . La, la, la, la. Where are you now? Where *are* you now? For they're hanging Danny Deever in the morning," he carolled, changing the subject.

He saw Jeeves, and suspended the painful performance.

"Hullo," he said. "*Quai hai*, my man. How are things?"

"Things are in a reasonably satisfactory state, sir."

"Where's Patch Rowcester?"

"His lordship is in the garden, sir."

"With Mrs. Spottsworth?"

"Yes, sir. Putting his fate to the test, to win or lose it all."

"You thought of something, then?"

"Yes, sir. The spider sequence."

"The how much?"

Captain Biggar listened attentively as Jeeves outlined the spider sequence, and when he had finished paid him a stately compliment.

"You'd do well out East, my boy."

"It is extremely kind of you to say so, sir."

"That is to say if that scheme was your own."

"It was, sir."

"Then you'd be just the sort of fellow we want in Kuala Lumpur. We need chaps like you, chaps who can use their brains. Can't leave brains all to the Dyaks. Makes the blighters get above themselves."

"The Dyaks are exceptionally intelligent, sir?"

"Are they! Let me tell you of something that happened to Tubby Frobisher and me one day when we ——" He broke off, and the world was deprived of another excellent story. Bill was coming through the French window.

A striking change had taken place in the ninth Earl in the few minutes since he had gone out through that window, a young man of spirit setting forth on a high adventure. His shoulders, as we have indicated, had then been square. Now they sagged like those of one who bears a heavy weight. His eyes were dull, his brow furrowed. The pride of the Rowcesters appeared to have packed up and withdrawn its support. No longer was there in his bearing any suggestion of that seventeenth-century ancestor who had infused so much of the party spirit into his decapitation on Tower Hill. The ancestor he most closely resembled now was the one who was caught cheating at cards by Charles James Fox at Wattier's in 1782.

"Well?" cried Captain Biggar.

Bill gave him a long, silent mournful look, and turned to Jeeves.

"Jeeves!"

"M'lord?"

"That spider sequence."

"Yes, m'lord?"

"I tried it."

"Yes, m'lord?"

"And things looked good for a moment. I detached the pendant."

"Yes, m'lord?"

"Captain Biggar was right. The clasp was loose. It came off."

Captain Biggar uttered a pleased exclamation in Swahili.

"Gimme," he said.

"I haven't got it. It slipped out of my hand."

"And fell?"

"And fell."

"You mean it's lying in the grass?"

"No," said Bill, with a sombre shake of the head. "It isn't lying in any ruddy grass. It went down the front of Mrs. Spottsworth's dress, and is now somewhere in the recesses of her costume."

14

Iᴛ is not often that one sees three good men struck all of a heap simultaneously, but anybody who had chanced to stroll into the living-room of Rowcester Abbey at this moment would have been able to observe that spectacle. To say that Bill's bulletin had had a shattering effect on his companions would be, if anything, to understate it. Captain Biggar was expressing his concern by pacing the room with whirling arms, while the fact that two of the hairs of his right eyebrow distinctly quivered showed how deeply Jeeves had been moved. Bill himself, crushed at last by the blows of Fate, appeared formally to have given up the struggle. He had slumped into a chair, and was sitting there looking boneless and despairing. All he needed was a long white beard, and the resemblance to King Lear on one of his bad mornings would have been complete.

Jeeves was the first to speak.

"Most disturbing, m'lord."

"Yes," said Bill dully. "Quite a nuisance, isn't it? You don't happen to have any little-known Asiatic poison on you, do you, Jeeves?"

"No, m'lord."

"A pity," said Bill. "I could have used it."

His young employer's distress pained Jeeves, and as it had always been his view that there was no anodyne for the human spirit, when bruised, like a spot of Marcus Aurelius, he searched in his mind for some suitable quotation from the Emperor's works. And he was just hesitating between 'Whatever may befall thee, it was preordained for thee from everlasting' and 'Nothing happens to any man which he is not fitted by nature to bear', both excellent, when Captain Biggar, who had been pouring out a rapid fire of ejaculations in some native dialect, suddenly reverted to English.

"*Doi wieng lek!*" he cried. "I've got it! Fricassee me with stewed mushrooms on the side, I see what you must do."

Bill looked up. His eyes were glazed, his manner listless.

"Do?" he said. "Me?"

"Yes, you."

"I'm sorry," said Bill. "I'm in no condition to do anything except possibly expire, regretted by all."

Captain Biggar snorted, and having snorted uttered a tchah, a pah and a bah.

"*Mun py nawn lap lao!*" he said impatiently. "You can dance, can't you?"

"Dance?"

"Preferably the Charleston. That's all I'm asking of you, a few simple steps of the Charleston."

Bill stirred slightly, like a corpse moving in its winding sheet. It was an acute spasm of generous indignation that caused him to do so. He was filled with what, in his opinion, was a justifiable resentment. Here he was, in the soup and going down for the third time, and this man came inviting him to dance before him as David danced before Saul. Assuming this to be merely the thin end of the wedge, one received the impression that in next to no time the White Hunter, if encouraged, would be calling for comic songs and conjuring tricks and imitations of footlight favourites who are familiar to you all. What, he asked himself bitterly, did the fellow think this was? The revival of Vaudeville? A village concert in aid of the church organ restoration fund?

Groping for words with which to express these thoughts, he found that the Captain was beginning to tell another of his stories. Like Marcus Aurelius, Kuala Lumpur's favourite son always seemed to have up his sleeve something apposite to the matter in hand, whatever that matter might be. But where the Roman Emperor, a sort of primitive Bob Hope or Groucho Marx, had contented himself with throwing off wisecracks, Captain Biggar preferred the narrative form.

"Yes, the Charleston," said Captain Biggar, "and I'll tell you why. I am thinking of the episode of Tubby Frobisher and the wife of the Greek consul. The recollection of it suddenly flashed upon me like a gleam of light from above."

He paused. A sense of something omitted, something left undone, was nagging at him. Then he saw why this was so. The whisky. He moved to the table and filled his glass.

"Whether it was Smyrna or Joppa or Stamboul where Tubby was stationed at the time of which I speak," he said, draining half the contents of his glass and coming back with the rest, "I'm afraid I can't tell you. As one grows older, one tends to forget these details. It may even have been Baghdad or half a dozen other places. I admit frankly that I have forgotten. But the point is that he was at some place somewhere and one night he attended a reception or a *soirée* or whatever they call these binges at one of the embassies. You know the sort of thing I mean. Fair women and brave men, all dolled up and dancing their ruddy heads off. And in due season it came to pass that Tubby found himself doing the Charleston with the wife of the Greek consul as his partner. I don't know if either of you have ever seen Tubby Frobisher dance the Charleston?"

"Neither his lordship nor myself have had the privilege of meeting Mr. Frobisher, sir," Jeeves reminded him courteously.

Captain Biggar stiffened.

"Major Frobisher, damn it."

"I beg your pardon, sir. Major Frobisher. Owing to our never having met him, the Major's technique when performing the Charleston is a sealed book to us."

"Oh?" Captain Biggar refilled his glass. "Well, his technique, as you call it, is vigorous. He does not spare himself. He is what in the old days would have been described as a three-collar man. By the time Tubby Frobisher has finished dancing the Charleston, his partner knows she has been in a fight, all right. And it was so on this occasion. He hooked on to the wife of the Greek consul and he jumped her up and he jumped her down, he whirled her about and he spun her round, he swung her here and he swung her there, and all of a sudden what do you think happened?"

"The lady had heart failure, sir?"

"No, the lady didn't have heart failure, but what occurred was enough to give it to all present at that gay affair. For, believe me or believe me not, there was a tinkling sound, and from inside her dress there began to descend to the floor silver forks, silver spoons and, Tubby assures me, a complete toilet set in tortoiseshell. It turned out that the female was a confirmed kleptomaniac and had been using the space between her dress and whatever she was wearing under her dress—I'm not a married man myself, so can't go into particulars—as a safe deposit."

"Embarrassing for Major Frobisher, sir."

Captain Biggar stared.

"For Tubby? Why? He hadn't been pinching the things, he was merely the instrument for their recovery. But don't tell me you've missed the whole point of my story, which is that I am convinced that if Patch Rowcester here were to dance the Charleston

with Mrs. Spottsworth with one tithe of Tubby Frobisher's deter-
mination and will to win, we'd soon rout that pendant out of its
retreat. Tubby would have had it in the open before the band had
played a dozen bars. And talking of that, we shall need music. Ah,
I see a gramophone over there in the corner. Excellent. Well? Do
you grasp the scheme?"

"Perfectly, sir. His lordship dances with Mrs. Spottsworth, and
in due course the pendant droppeth as the gentle rain from heaven
upon the place beneath."

"Exactly. What do you think of the idea?"

Jeeves referred the question to a higher court.

"What does your lordship think of it?" he asked deferentially.

"Eh?" said Bill. "What?"

Captain Biggar barked sharply.

"You mean you haven't been listening? Well, of all the——"

Jeeves intervened.

"In the circumstances, sir, his lordship may, I think, be excused
for being distrait," he said reprovingly. "You can see from his
lordship's lack-lustre eye that the native hue of his resolution is
sicklied o'er with the pale cast of thought. Captain Biggar's suggestion is, m'lord, that your lordship shall invite Mrs. Spottsworth
to join you in performing the dance known as the Charleston. This,
if your lordship infuses sufficient vigour into the steps, will result
in the pendant becoming dislodged and falling to the ground,
whence it can readily be recovered and placed in your lordship's
pocket."

It was perhaps a quarter of a minute before the gist of these
remarks penetrated to Bill's numbed mind, but when it did, the
effect was electric. His eyes brightened, his spine stiffened. It was
plain that hope had dawned, and was working away once more at
the old stand. As he rose from his chair, jauntily and with the air
of a man who is ready for anything, he might have been that
debonair ancestor of his who in the days of the Restoration had by
his dash and gallantry won from the ladies of King Charles the
Second's Court the affectionate sobriquet of Tabasco Rowcester.

"Lead me to her!" he said, and his voice rang out clear and
resonant. "Lead me to her, that is all I ask, and leave the rest to
me."

But it was not necessary, as it turned out, to lead him to Mrs.
Spottsworth, for at this moment she came in through the French
window with her Pekinese dog Pomona in her arms.

Pomona, on seeing the assembled company, gave vent to a series of piercing shrieks. It sounded as if she were being torn asunder by red-hot pincers, but actually this was her method of expressing joy. In moments of ecstasy she always screamed partly like a lost soul and partly like a scalded cat.

Jill came running out of the library, and Mrs. Spottsworth calmed her fears.

"It's nothing, dear," she said. "She's just excited. But I wish you would put her in my room, if you are going upstairs. Would it be troubling you too much?"

"Not at all," said Jill aloofly.

She went out, carrying Pomona, and Bill advanced on Mrs. Spottsworth.

"Shall we dance?" he said.

Mrs. Spottsworth was surprised. On the rustic seat just now, especially in the moments following the disappearance of her pendant, she had found her host's mood markedly on the Byronic side. She could not readily adjust herself to this new spirit of gaiety.

"You want to *dance*?"

"Yes, with *you*," said Bill, infusing into his manner a wealth of Restoration gallantry. "It'll be like the old days at Cannes."

Mrs. Spottsworth was a shrewd woman. She had not failed to observe Captain Biggar lurking in the background, and it seemed to her that an admirable opportunity had presented itself of rousing the fiend that slept in him . . . far too soundly, in her opinion. What it was that was slowing up the White Hunter in his capacity of wooer, she did not know: but what she did know was that there is nothing that so lights a fire under a laggard lover as the spectacle of the woman he loves treading the measure in the arms of another man, particularly another man as good-looking as William, Earl of Rowcester.

"Yes, won't it!" she said, all sparkle and enthusiasm. "How well I remember those days! Lord Rowcester dances so wonderfully," she added, addressing Captain Biggar and imparting to him a piece of first-hand information which, of course, he would have been sorry to have missed. "I love dancing. The one unpunished rapture left on earth."

"What ho!" said Bill, concurring. "The old Charleston . . . do you remember it?"

"You bet I do."

"Put a Charleston record on the gramophone, Jeeves."

"Very good, m'lord."

When Jill returned from depositing Pomona in Mrs. Spottsworth's sleeping quarters, only Jeeves, Bill and Mrs. Spottsworth were present in the living-room, for at the very outset of the proceedings Captain Biggar, unable to bear the sight before him, had plunged through the French window into the silent night.

The fact that it was he himself who had suggested this distressing exhibition, recalling, as it did in his opinion the worst excesses of the Carmagnole of the French Revolution combined with some of the more risqué features of native dances he had seen in Equatorial Africa, did nothing to assuage the darkness of his mood. The frogs on the lawn, which he was now pacing with a black scowl on his face, were beginning to get the illusion that it was raining number eleven boots.

His opinion of the Charleston, as rendered by his host and the woman he loved, was one which Jill found herself sharing. As she stood watching from the doorway, she was conscious of much the same rising feeling of nausea which had afflicted the White Hunter when listening to the exchanges on the rustic seat. Possibly there was nothing in the way in which Bill was comporting himself that rendered him actually liable to arrest, but she felt very strongly that some form of action should have been taken by the police. It was her view that there ought to have been a law.

Nothing is more difficult than to describe in words a Charleston danced by, on the one hand, a woman who loves dancing Charlestons and throws herself right into the spirit of them, and, on the other hand, by a man desirous of leaving no stone unturned in order to dislodge from some part of his associate's anatomy a diamond pendant which has lodged there. It will be enough, perhaps, to say that if Major Frobisher had happened to walk into the room at this moment, he would instantly have been reminded of old days in Smyrna or Joppa or Stamboul or possibly Baghdad. Mrs. Spottsworth he would have compared favourably with the wife of the Greek consul, while Bill he would have patted on the back, recognizing his work as fully equal, if not superior, to his own.

Rory and Monica, coming out of the library, were frankly amazed.

"Good heavens!" said Monica.

"The old boy cuts quite a rug, does he not?" said Rory. "Come, girl, let us join the revels."

He put his arm about Monica's waist, and the action became general. Jill, unable to bear the degrading spectacle any longer, turned and went out. As she made her way to her room, she was thinking unpleasant thoughts of her betrothed. It is never agreeable for an idealistic girl to discover that she has linked her lot with a libertine, and it was plain to her now that William, Earl of Rowcester, was a debauchee whose correspondence course might have been taken with advantage by Casanova, Don Juan and the rowdier Roman Emperors.

"When I dance," said Mrs. Spottsworth, cutting, like her partner, quite a rug, "I don't know I've got feet."

Monica winced.

"If you danced with Rory, you'd know you've got feet. It's the way he jumps on and off that gets you down."

"Ouch!" said Mrs. Spottsworth suddenly. Bill had just lifted her and brought her down with a bump which would have excited Tubby Frobisher's generous admiration, and she was now standing rubbing her leg. "I've twisted something," she said, hobbling to a chair.

"I'm not surprised," said Monica, "the way Bill was dancing."

"Oh, gee, I hope it is just a twist and not my sciatica come back. I suffer so terribly from sciatica, especially if I'm in a place that's at all damp."

Incredible as it may seem, Rory did not say 'Like Rowcester Abbey, what?' and go on to speak of the garden which, in the winter months, was at the bottom of the river. He was peering down at an object lying on the floor.

"Hullo," he said. "What's this? Isn't this pendant yours, Mrs. Spottsworth?"

"Oh, thank you," said Mrs. Spottsworth. "Yes, it's mine. It must have . . . Ouch!" she said, breaking off, and writhed in agony once more.

Monica was all concern.

"You must get straight to bed, Rosalinda."

"I guess I should."

"With a nice hot-water bottle."

"Yes."

"Rory will help you upstairs."

"Charmed," said Rory. "But why do people always speak of a 'nice' hot-water bottle? We at Harrige's say 'nasty' hot-water bottle. Our electric pads have rendered the hot-water bottle obsolete. Three speeds . . . Autumn Glow, Spring Warmth and Mae West."

They moved to the door, Mrs. Spottsworth leaning heavily on his arm. They passed out, and Bill, who had followed them with a bulging eye, threw up his hands in a wide gesture of despair.

"Jeeves!"

"M'lord?"

"This is the end!"

"Yes, m'lord."

"She's gone to ground."

"Yes, m'lord."

"Accompanied by the pendant."

"Yes, m'lord."

"So unless you have any suggestions for getting her out of that room, we're sunk. Have you any suggestions?"

"Not at the moment, m'lord."

"I didn't think you would have. After all, you're human, and the problem is one which is not within . . . what, Jeeves?"

"The scope of human power, m'lord."

"Exactly. Do you know what I am going to do?"

"No, m'lord?"

"Go to bed, Jeeves. Go to bed and try to sleep and forget. Not that I have the remotest chance of getting to sleep, with every nerve in my body sticking out a couple of inches and curling at the ends."

"Possibly if your lordship were to count sheep——"

"You think that would work?"

"It is a widely recognized specific, m'lord."

"H'm." Bill considered. "Well, no harm in trying it. Good night, Jeeves."

"Good night, m'lord."

* 15 *

EXCEPT for the squeaking of mice behind the wainscoting and an occasional rustling sound as one of the bats in the chimney stirred uneasily in its sleep, Rowcester Abbey lay hushed and still. 'Twas now the very witching time of night, and in the Blue Room Rory and Monica, pleasantly fatigued after the activities of the day, slumbered peacefully. In the Queen Elizabeth Room Mrs. Spottsworth, Pomona in her basket at her side, had also dropped off. In the Anne Boleyn Room Captain Biggar, the good man taking his rest, was dreaming of old days on the Me Wang river, which, we need scarcely inform our public, is a tributary of the larger and more crocodile-infested Wang Me.

Jill, in the Clock Room, was still awake, staring at the ceiling with hot eyes, and Bill, counting sheep in the Henry the Eighth Room, had also failed to find oblivion. The specific recommended by Jeeves might be widely recognized but so far it had done nothing toward enabling him to knit up the ravelled sleeve of care.

"Eight hundred and twenty-two," murmured Bill. "Eight hundred and twenty-three. Eight hundred and ——"

He broke off, leaving the eight hundred and twenty-fourth sheep, an animal with a more than usually vacuous expression on its face, suspended in the air into which it had been conjured up. Someone had knocked on the door, a knock so soft and deferential that it could have proceeded from the knuckle of only one man. It was consequently without surprise that a moment later he perceived Jeeves entering.

"Your lordship will excuse me," said Jeeves courteously. "I would not have disturbed your lordship, had I not, listening at the door, gathered from your lordship's remarks that the stratagem which I proposed had proved unsuccessful."

"No, it hasn't worked yet," said Bill, "but come in, Jeeves, come in." He would have been glad to see anything that was not a sheep. "Don't tell me," he said, starting as he noted the gleam of intelligence in his visitor's eye, "that you've thought of something?"

"Yes, m'lord, I am happy to say that I fancy I have found a solution to the problem which confronted us."

"Jeeves, you're a marvel!"

"Thank you very much, m'lord."

"I remember Bertie Wooster saying to me once that there was no crisis which you were unable to handle."

"Mr. Wooster has always been far too flattering, m'lord."

"Nonsense. Not nearly flattering enough. If you have really put your finger on a way of overcoming the superhuman difficulties in our path——"

"I feel convinced that I have, m'lord."

Bill quivered inside his mauve pyjama jacket.

"Think well, Jeeves," he urged. "Somehow or other we have got to get Mrs. Spottsworth out of her room for a lapse of time sufficient to enable me to bound in, find that pendant, scoop it up and bound out again, all this without a human eye resting upon me. Unless I have completely misinterpreted your words owing to having suffered a nervous breakdown from counting sheep, you seem to be suggesting that you can do this. How? That is the question that springs to the lips. With mirrors?"

Jeeves did not speak for a moment. A pained look had come into his finely-chiselled face. It was as though he had suddenly seen some sight which was occasioning his distress.

"Excuse me, m'lord. I am reluctant to take what is possibly a liberty on my part——"

"Carry on, Jeeves. You have our ear. What is biting you?"

"It is your pyjamas, m'lord. Had I been aware that your lordship was in the habit of sleeping in mauve pyjamas, I would have advised against it. Mauve does not become your lordship. I was once compelled, in his best interests, to speak in a similar vein to Mr. Wooster, who at that time was also a mauve-pyjama addict."

Bill found himself at a loss.

"How have we got on to the subject of pyjamas?" he asked, wonderingly.

"They thrust themselves on the notice, m'lord. That very aggressive purple. If your lordship would be guided by me and substitute a quiet blue or possibly a light pistachio green——"

"Jeeves!"

"M'lord?"

"This is no time to be prattling of pyjamas."

"Very good, m'lord."

"As a matter of fact, I rather fancy myself in mauve. But that, as I say, is neither here nor there. Let us postpone the discussion to a more suitable moment. I will, however, tell you this. If you really have something to suggest with reference to that pendant and that something brings home the bacon, you may take these mauve pyjamas and raze them to the ground and sow salt on the foundations."

"Thank you very much, m'lord."

"It will be a small price to pay for your services. Well, now that you've got me all worked up, tell me more. What's the good news? What is this scheme of yours?"

"A quite simple one, m'lord. It is based on——"

Bill uttered a cry.

"Don't tell me. Let me guess. The psychology of the individual?"

"Precisely, m'lord."

Bill drew in his breath sharply.

"I thought as much. Something told me that was it. Many a time and oft, exchanging dry Martinis with Bertie Wooster in the bar of the Drones Club, I have listened to him, rapt, as he spoke of you and the psychology of the individual. He said that, once you get your teeth into the psychology of the individual, it's all over except chucking one's hat in the air and doing Spring dances. Proceed, Jeeves. You interest me strangely. The individual whose psychology you have been brooding on at the present juncture is, I take it, Mrs. Spottsworth? Am I right or wrong, Jeeves?"

"Perfectly correct, m'lord. Has it occurred to your lordship what is Mrs. Spottsworth's principal interest, the thing uppermost in the lady's mind?"

Bill gaped.

"You haven't come here at two in the morning to suggest that I dance the Charleston with her again?"

"Oh, no, m'lord."

"Well, when you spoke of her principal interest——"

"There is another facet of Mrs. Spottsworth's character which you have overlooked, m'lord. I concede that she is an enthusiastic Charleston performer, but what principally occupies her thoughts is psychical research. Since her arrival at the Abbey, she has not ceased to express a hope that she may be granted the experience of seeing the spectre of Lady Agatha. It was that that I had in mind when I informed your lordship that I had formulated a scheme for obtaining the pendant, based on the psychology of the individual."

Bill sank back on the pillows, a disappointed man.

"No, Jeeves," he said. "I won't do it."

"M'lord?"

"I see where you're heading. You want me to dress up in a farthingale and wimple and sneak into Mrs. Spottsworth's room, your contention being that if she wakes and sees me, she will simply say 'Ah, the ghost of Lady Adela', and go to sleep again. It can't be done, Jeeves. Nothing will induce me to dress up in women's clothes, not even in such a deserving cause as this one. I might stretch a point and put on the old moustache and black patch."

"I would not advocate it, m'lord. Even on the racecourse I have observed clients, on seeing your lordship, start back with visible concern. A lady, discovering such an apparition in her room, might quite conceivably utter a piercing scream."

Bill threw his hands up with a despondent groan.

"Well, there you are, then. The thing's off. Your scheme falls to the ground and becomes null and void."

"No, m'lord. Your lordship has not, if I may say so, grasped the substance of the plan I am putting forward. The essential at which one aims is the inducing of Mrs. Spottsworth to leave her room, thus rendering it possible for your lordship to enter and secure the pendant. I propose now, with your lordship's approval, to knock on Mrs. Spottsworth's door and request the loan of a bottle of smelling salts."

Bill clutched at his hair.

"You said, Jeeves?"

"Smelling salts, m'lord."

Bill shook his head.

"Counting those sheep has done something to me," he said. "My hearing has become affected. It sounded to me just as if you had said 'Smelling salts'."

"I did, m'lord. I would explain that I required them in order to restore your lordship to consciousness."

"There again. I could have sworn that I heard you say 'restore your lordship to consciousness'."

"Precisely, m'lord. Your lordship has sustained a severe shock. Happening to be in the vicinity of the ruined chapel at about the hour of midnight, your lordship observed the wraith of Lady Agatha and was much overcome. How your lordship contrived to totter back to your room, your lordship will never know, but I found your lordship there in a what appeared to be a coma and immediately applied to Mrs. Spottsworth for the loan of her smelling salts."

Bill was still at a loss.

"I don't get the gist, Jeeves."

"If I might elucidate my meaning still further, m'lord. The thought I had in mind was that, learning that Lady Agatha was, if I may so term it, on the wing, Mrs. Spottsworth's immediate reaction would be an intense desire to hasten to the ruined chapel in order to observe the manifestation for herself. I would offer to escort her thither, and during her absence . . ."

It is never immediately that the ordinary man, stunned by some revelation of genius, is able to find words with which to express his emotion. When Alexander Graham Bell, meeting a friend one morning in the year 1876, said 'Oh, hullo, George, heard the latest? I invented the telephone yesterday', it is probable that the friend merely shuffled his feet in silence. It was the same with Bill now. He could not speak. He lay there dumbly, while remorse flooded over him that he could ever have doubted this man. It was just as Bertie Wooster had so often said. Let this fish-fed master-mind get his teeth into the psychology of the individual, and it was all over except chucking your hat in the air and doing Spring dances.

"Jeeves," he began, at length finding speech, but Jeeves was shimmering through the door.

"Your smelling salts, m'lord," he said, turning his head on the threshold. "If your lordship will excuse me."

It was perhaps two minutes, though to Bill it seemed longer, before he returned, bearing a small bottle.

"Well?" said Bill eagerly.

"Everything has gone according to plan, m'lord. The lady's reactions were substantially as I had anticipated. Mrs. Spottsworth, on receiving my communication, displayed immediate interest. Is your lordship familiar with the expression 'Jiminy Christmas!'?"

"No, I don't think I ever heard it. You don't mean 'Merry Christmas'?"

"No, m'lord. 'Jiminy Christmas!' It was what Mrs. Spottsworth observed on receiving the information that the phantasm of Lady Agatha was to be seen in the ruined chapel. The words, I gathered, were intended to convey surprise and elation. She assured me that it would take her but a brief time to hop into a dressing-gown and that at the conclusion of that period she would be with me with, I understood her to say, her hair in a braid. I am to return in a moment and accompany her to the scene of the manifestation. I will leave the door open a few inches, so that your lordship, by applying your lordship's eye to the crack, may be able to see us depart. As soon as we have descended the staircase, I would advocate instant action, for I need scarcely remind your lordship that time is——"

"Of the essence? No, you certainly don't have to tell me that. You remember what you were saying about cheetahs?"

"With reference to their speed of foot, m'lord?"

"That's right. Half a mile in forty-five seconds, I think you said?"

"Yes, m'lord."

"Well, the way I shall move would leave the nippiest cheetah standing at the post."

"That will be highly satisfactory, m'lord. I, on my side, may mention that on the dressing-table in Mrs. Spottsworth's room I observed a small jewel-case, which I have no doubt contains the pendant. The dressing-table is immediately beneath the window. Your lordship will have no difficulty in locating it."

He was right, as always. It was the first thing that Bill saw when, having watched the little procession of two out of sight down the stairs, he hastened along the corridor to the Queen Elizabeth Room. There, as Jeeves had stated, was the dressing-table. On it was the small jewel-case of which he had spoken. And in that jewel-case, as he opened it with shaking hands, Bill saw the pendant. Hastily he slipped it into the pocket of his pyjamas, and was turning to leave, when the silence, which had been complete but for his heavy breathing, was shattered by a series of dreadful screams.

Reference has been made earlier to the practice of the dog Pomona of shrieking loudly to express the ecstasy she always felt on beholding a friend or even what looked to her like a congenial stranger. It was ecstasy that was animating her now. In the course of that session on the rustic seat, when Bill had done his cooing, she had taken an immediate fancy to her host, as all dogs did. Meeting him now in this informal fashion, just at a moment when she had been trying to reconcile herself to the solitude which she so disliked, she made no attempt to place any bounds on her self-expression.

Screams sufficient in number and volume to have equipped a dozen Baronets stabbed in the back in libraries burst from her lips and their effect on Bill was devastating. The author of *The Hunting Of The Snark* says of one of his protagonists in a powerful passage:

> 'So great was his fright
> That his waistcoat turned white'

and the experience through which he was passing nearly caused Bill's mauve pyjamas to do the same.

Though fond of Pomona, he did not linger to fraternize. He shot out of the door at a speed which would have had the most athletic cheetah shrugging its shoulders helplessly, and arrived in the corridor just as Jill, roused from sleep by those awful cries, came out of the Clock Room. She watched him steal softly into the Henry the Eighth Room, and thought in bitter mood that a more suitable spot for him could scarcely have been found.

It was some quarter of an hour later, as Bill, lying in bed, was murmuring 'Nine hundred and ninety-eight . . . Nine hundred and ninety-nine . . . One thousand . . ." that Jeeves entered.

He was carrying a salver.

On that salver was a ring.

"I encountered Miss Wyvern in the corridor a few moments ago, m'lord," he said. "She desired me to give this to your lordship."

* 16 *

WYVERN HALL, the residence of Colonel Aubrey Wyvern, father of Jill and Chief Constable of the county of Southmolton-shire, lay across the river from Rowcester Abbey, and on the following afternoon Colonel Wyvern, having worked his way scowlingly through a most inferior lunch, stumped out of the dining-room and went to his study and rang for his butler. And in due course the butler entered, tripping over the rug with a muffled 'Whoops!', his invariable practice when crossing any threshold.

Colonel Wyvern was short and stout, and this annoyed him, for he would have preferred to be tall and slender. But if his personal appearance gave him pangs of discomfort from time to time, they were as nothing compared to the pangs the personal appearance of his butler gave him. In England today the householder in the country has to take what he can get in the way of domestic help, and all Colonel Wyvern had been able to get was the scrapings and scourings of the local parish school. Bulstrode, the major-domo of Wyvern Hall, was a skinny stripling of some sixteen summers, on whom Nature in her bounty had bestowed so many pimples that there was scarcely room on his face for the vacant grin which habitually adorned it.

He was grinning now, and once again, as always happened at these staff conferences, his overlord was struck by the closeness of the lad's resemblance to a half-witted goldfish peering out of a bowl.

"Bulstrode," he said, with a parade-ground rasp in his voice.

"Yus?" replied the butler affably.

At another moment, Colonel Wyvern would have had something to say on the subject of this unconventional verbal approach but today he was after bigger game. His stomach was still sending up complaints to the front office about the lunch, and he wanted to see the cook.

"Bulstrode," he said, "bring the cook to me."

The cook, conducted into the presence, proved also to be one of the younger set. Her age was fifteen. She bustled in, her pigtails

136

swinging behind her, and Colonel Wyvern gave her an unpleasant look.

"Trelawny!" he said.

"Yus?" said the cook.

This time there was no reticence on the part of the Chief Constable. The Wyverns did not as a rule war upon women, but there are times when chivalry is impossible.

"Don't say 'Yus?', you piefaced little excrescence," he thundered. "Say 'Yes, sir?', and say it in a respectful and soldierly manner, coming smartly to attention with the thumbs on the seam of the trousers. Trelawny, that lunch you had the temerity to serve up today was an insult to me and a disgrace to anyone daring to call herself a cook, and I have sent for you to inform you that if there is any more of this spirit of slackness and *laissez faire* on your part . . ." Colonel Wyvern paused. The 'I'll tell your mother', with which he had been about to conclude his sentence, seemed to him to lack a certain something. "You'll hear of it," he said and, feeling that even this was not as good as he could have wished, infused such vigour and venom into his description of underdone chicken, watery brussels sprouts and potatoes you couldn't get a fork into that a weaker girl might well have wilted.

But the Trelawnys were made of tough stuff. They did not quail in the hour of peril. The child met his eye with iron resolution, and came back strongly.

"Hitler!" she said, putting out her tongue.

The Chief Constable started.

"Did you call me Hitler?"

"Yus, I did."

"Well, don't do it again," said Colonel Wyvern sternly. "You may go, Trelawny."

Trelawny went, with her nose in the air, and Colonel Wyvern addressed himself to Bulstrode.

A proud man is never left unruffled when worsted in a verbal duel with a cook, especially a cook aged fifteen with pigtails, and in the Chief Constable's manner as he turned on his butler there was more than a suggestion of a rogue elephant at the height of its fever. For some minutes he spoke well and forcefully, with particular reference to the other's habit of chewing his sweet ration while waiting at table, and when at length he was permitted to follow Evangeline Trelawny to the lower regions in which they had their being, Bulstrode, if not actually shaking in every limb, was at any rate subdued enough to omit to utter his customary 'Whoops!' when tripping over the rug.

He left the Chief Constable, though feeling a little better after having cleansed his bosom of the perilous stuff that weighs upon the soul, still definitely despondent. 'Ichabod', he was saying to himself, and he meant it. In the golden age before the social revolution, he was thinking, a gaping, pimpled tripper over rugs like this Bulstrode would have been a lowly hall-boy, if that. It revolted a Tory of the old school's finer feelings to have to regard such a blot on the Southmoltonshire scene in the sacred light of a butler.

He thought nostalgically of his young manhood in London at the turn of the century and of the vintage butlers he had been wont to encounter in those brave days . . . butlers who weighed two hundred and fifty pounds on the hoof, butlers with three chins and bulging abdomens, butlers with large, gooseberry eyes and that austere, supercilious, butlerine manner which has passed away so completely from the degenerate world of the nineteen-fifties. Butlers had been butlers then in the deepest and holiest sense of the word. Now they were mere chinless boys who sucked toffee and said 'Yus?' when you spoke to them.

It was almost inevitable that a man living so near to Rowcester Abbey and starting to brood on butlers should find his thoughts turning in the direction of the Abbey's principal ornament, and it was with a warm glow that Colonel Wyvern now began to think of Jeeves. Jeeves had made a profound impression on him. Jeeves, in his opinion, was the goods. Young Rowcester himself was a fellow the Colonel, never very fond of his juniors, could take or leave alone, but this man of his, this Jeeves, he had recognized from their first meeting as something special. Out of the night that covered the Chief Constable, black as the pit—after that disturbing scene with Evangeline Trelawny—from pole to pole, there shone a sudden gleam of light. He himself might have his Bulstrode, but at least he could console himself with the thought that his daughter was marrying a man with a butler in the fine old tradition on his payroll. It put heart into him. It made him feel that this was not such a bad little old world, after all.

He mentioned this to Jill when she came in a moment later, looking cold and proud, and Jill tilted her chin and looked colder and prouder. She might have been a Snow Queen or something of that sort.

"I am not going to marry Lord Rowcester," she said curtly.

It seemed to Colonel Wyvern that his child must be suffering from some form of amnesia, and he set himself to jog her memory.

"Yes, you are," he reminded her. "It was in *The Times*. I saw it with my own eyes. The engagement is announced between——"

"I have broken off the engagement."

That little gleam of light of which we were speaking a moment ago, the one we showed illuminating Colonel Wyvern's darkness, went out with a pop, like a stage moon that has blown a fuse. He stared incredulously.

"Broken off the engagement?"

"I am never going to speak to Lord Rowcester again."

"Don't be an ass," said Colonel Wyvern. "Of course you are. Not going to speak to him again? I never heard such nonsense. I suppose what's happened is that you've had one of these lovers' tiffs."

Jill did not intend to allow without protest what was probably the world's greatest tragedy since the days of Romeo and Juliet to be described in this inadequate fashion. One really must take a little trouble to find the *mot juste*.

"It was not a lovers' tiff," she said, all the woman in her flashing from her eyes. "If you want to know why I broke off the engagement, it was because of the abominable way he has been behaving with Mrs. Spottsworth."

Colonel Wyvern put a finger to his brow.

"Spottsworth? Spottsworth? Ah, yes. That's the American woman you were telling me about."

"The American trollop," corrected Jill coldly.

"Trollop?" said Colonel Wyvern, intrigued.

"That was what I said."

"Why do you call her that? Did you catch them—er—trolloping?"

"Yes, I did."

"Good gracious!"

Jill swallowed once or twice, as if something jagged in her throat was troubling her.

"It all seems to have started," she said, speaking in that toneless voice which had made such a painful impression on Bill, "in Cannes some years ago. Apparently she and Lord Rowcester used to swim together at Eden Roc and go for long drives in the moonlight. And you know what that sort of thing leads to."

"I do indeed," said Colonel Wyvern with animation, and was about to embark on an anecdote of his interesting past, when Jill went on, still speaking in that same strange, toneless voice.

"She arrived at the Abbey yesterday. The story that has been put out is that Monica Carmoyle met her in New York and invited her to stay, but I have no doubt that the whole thing was arranged between her and Lord Rowcester, because it was obvious how matters stood between them. No sooner had she appeared than he was all over her . . . making love to her in the garden, dancing with her like a cat on hot bricks, and," said Jill nonchalantly, wearing the mask like the Mrs. Fish who had so diverted Captain Biggar by doing the can-can in her step-ins in Kenya, "coming out of her room at two o'clock in the morning in mauve pyjamas."

Colonel Wyvern choked. He had been about to try to heal the rift by saying that it was quite possible for a man to exchange a few civil remarks with a woman in a garden and while away the long evening by partnering her in the dance and still not be in any way culpable, but this statement wiped the words from his lips.

"Coming out of her room in mauve pyjamas?"

"Yes."

"*Mauve* pyjamas?"

"Bright mauve."

"God bless my soul!"

A club acquaintance, annoyed by the eccentricity of the other's bridge game, had once told Colonel Wyvern that he looked like a retired member of Sanger's troupe of midgets who for years had been doing himself too well on the starchy foods, and this was in a measure true. He was, as we have said, short and stout. But when the call to action came, he could triumph over his brevity of stature and rotundity of waistcoat and become a figure of dignity and menace. It was an impressive Chief Constable who strode across the room and rang the bell for Bulstrode.

"Yus?" said Bulstrode.

Colonel Wyvern choked down the burning words he would have liked to utter. He told himself that he must conserve his energies.

"Bulstrode," he said, "bring me my horsewhip."

Down in the forest of pimples on the butler's face something stirred. It was a look of guilt.

"It's gorn," he mumbled.

Colonel Wyvern stared.

"Gone? What do you mean, gone? Gone where?"

Bulstrode choked. He had been hoping that this investigation might have been avoided. Something had told him that it would prove embarrassing.

"To the mender's. To be mended. It got cracked."

"Cracked?"

"Yus," said Bulstrode, in his emotion adding the unusual word 'Sir'. "I was cracking it in the stable yard, and it cracked. So I took it to the mender's."

Colonel Wyvern pointed an awful finger at the door.

"Get out, you foul blot," he said. "I'll talk to you later." Seating himself at his desk, as he always did when he wished to think, he drummed his fingers on the arm of his chair. "I'll have to borrow young Rowcester's," he said at length, clicking his tongue in evident annoyance. "Infernally awkward, calling on a fellow you're going to horsewhip and having to ask him for the loan of his horsewhip to do it with. Still, there it is," said Colonel Wyvern philosophically. "That's how it goes."

He was a man who could always adjust himself to circumstances.

17

LUNCH at Rowcester Abbey had been a much more agreeable function than lunch at Wyvern Hall, on a different plane altogether. Where Colonel Wyvern had been compelled to cope with the distressing efforts of a pigtailed incompetent apparently under the impression that she was catering for a covey of buzzards in the Gobi Desert, the revellers at the Abbey had been ministered to by an expert. Earlier in this chronicle passing reference was made to the virtuosity of Bill's O.C. Kitchen, the richly gifted Mrs. Piggott, and in dishing up the midday meal today she had in no way fallen short of her high ideals. Three of the four celebrants at the table had found the food melting in their mouths and had downed it with cries of appreciation.

The exception was the host himself, in whose mouth it had turned to ashes. What with one thing and another—the instability of his financial affairs, last night's burglarious interlude and its devastating sequel, the shattering of his romance—Bill was far from being the gayest of all that gay company. In happier days he had sometimes read novels in which characters were described as pushing their food away untasted, and had often wondered, being a man who enjoyed getting his calories, how they could have brought themselves to do it. But at the meal which was now coming to an end he had been doing it himself, and, as we say, what little nourishment he had contrived to take had turned to ashes in his mouth. He had filled in the time mostly by crumbling bread, staring wildly and jumping like a galvanized frog when spoken to. A cat in a strange alley would have been more at its ease.

Nor had the conversation at the table done anything to restore his equanimity. Mrs. Spottsworth would keep bringing it round to the subject of Captain Biggar, regretting his absence from the feast, and each mention of the White Hunter's name had had a seismic effect on his sensitive conscience. She did it again now.

"Captain Biggar was telling me——" she began, and Rory uttered one of his jolly laughs.

"He was, was he?" he said in his tactful way. "Well, I hope you didn't believe him."

Mrs. Spottsworth stiffened. She sensed a slur on the man she loved.

"I beg your pardon?"

"Awful liar, that chap."

"Why do you say that, Sir Roderick?"

"I was thinking of those yarns of his at dinner last night."

"They were perfectly true."

"Not a bit of it," said Rory buoyantly. "Don't you let him pull your leg, my dear Mrs. Dogsbody. All these fellows from out East are the most frightful liars. It's due, I believe, to the ultra-violet rays of the sun in those parts. They go out without their solar topees, and it does something to them. I have this from an authoritative source. One of them used to come to headquarters a lot when I was in the Guns, Pistols and Ammunition, and we became matey. And one night, when in his cups, he warned me not to swallow a single word any of them said. 'Look at me', he reasoned. 'Did you ever hear a chap tell the ghastly lies I do? Why, I haven't spoken the truth since I was so high. And so low are standards east of Suez that my nickname out there is George Washington'."

"Coffee is served in the living-room, m'lord," said Jeeves, intervening in his polished way and averting what promised, judging from the manner in which Mrs. Spottsworth's eyes had begun to glitter, to develop into an ugly brawl.

Following his guests into the living-room, Bill was conscious of a growing sense of uneasiness and alarm. He had not supposed that anything could have increased his mental discomfort, but Rory's words had done so a hundredfold. As he lowered himself into a chair, accepted a cup of coffee and spilled it over his trousers, one more vulture had added itself to the little group already gnawing at his bosom. For the first time he had begun to question the veracity of Captain Biggar's story of the pendant, and at the thought of what he had let himself in for if that story had not been true his imagination boggled.

Dimly he was aware that Rory and Monica had collected all the morning papers and were sitting surrounded by them their faces grave and tense. The sands were running out. Less than an hour from now the Derby would be run, and soon, if ever, they must decide how their wagers were to be placed.

"*Racing News*," said Monica, calling the meeting to order. "What does the *Racing News* say, Rory?"

Rory studied that sheet in his slow, thorough way.

"Lot of stuff about the Guineas form. Perfect rot, all of it. You can't go by the Guineas. Too many unknowns. If you want my considered opinion, there's nothing in sight to beat Taj Mahal. The Aga has the mares, and that's what counts. The sires don't begin to matter compared with the mares."

"I'm glad to hear you pay this belated tribute to my sex."

"Yes, I think for my two quid it's Taj Mahal on the nose."

"That settles Taj Mahal for me. Whenever you bet on them, they start running backwards. Remember that dog-race."

Rory was obliged to yield this point.

"I admit my nominee let the side down on that occasion," he said. "But when a real rabbit gets loose on a dog track, it's bound to cause a bit of confusion. Taj Mahal gets my two o'goblins."

"I thought your money was going on Oratory."

"Oratory is my outsider bet, ten bob each way."

"Well, here's another hunch for you. Escalator."

"Escalator?"

"Wasn't H's the first store to have escalators?"

"By jove, yes. We've got the cup, you know. Our safety-landing device has enabled us to clip three seconds off the record. The Oxford Street boys are livid. I must look into this Escalator matter."

"Lester Piggott is riding it."

"That settles it. L. Piggott is the name of the chap stationed in the Trunks, Bags and Suit-cases, as fine a man as ever punched a time-clock. I admit his L stands for Lancelot, but that's a good enough omen for me."

Monica looked across at Mrs. Spottsworth.

"I suppose you think we're crazy, Rosalinda?"

Mrs. Spottsworth smiled indulgently.

"Of course not, dear. This brings back the old days with Mr. Bessemer. Racing was all he ever thought of. We spent our honeymoon at Sheepshead Bay. It's the Derby, is it, you're so interested in?"

"Just our silly little annual flutter. We don't bet high. Can't afford to. We have to watch the pennies."

"Rigidly," said Rory. He chuckled amusedly, struck by a whimsical idea. "I was just thinking," he went on in explanation of his mirth, "that the smart thing for me to have done would have been to stick to that pendant of yours I picked up last night and go off to London with it and pawn it, thus raising a bit of . . . Yes, old man?"

Bill swallowed.

"I didn't speak."

"I thought you did."

"No, just a hiccup."

"To which," Rory conceded, "you were fully entitled. If a man can't hiccup in his own house, in whose house can he hiccup? Well, summing up, Taj Mahal two quid. Escalator ten bob each way. I'll go and send off my wire." He paused. "But wait. Is it not rash to commit oneself without consulting Jeeves?"

"Why Jeeves?"

"My dear Moke, what that man doesn't know about form isn't worth knowing. You should have heard him yesterday when I asked him if he had any views on the respective contestants in England's premier classic race. He just stood there rattling off horses and times and records as if he were the Archbishop of Canterbury."

Monica was impressed.

"I didn't know he was as hot as that. Are there no limits to the powers of this wonder man? We'll go and confer with him at once."

They hurried out, and Bill, having cleared his throat, said 'Er'.

Mrs. Spottsworth looked up inquiringly.

"Er, Rosie. That pendant of yours. The one Rory was speaking of."

"Yes?"

"I was admiring it last night."

"It's nice, isn't it?"

"Beautiful. You didn't have it at Cannes, did you?"

"No. I hadn't met Mr. Spottsworth then. It was a present from him."

Bill leaped. His worst suspicions had been confirmed.

"A present from Mr. Sp——?" he gasped.

Mrs. Spottsworth laughed.

"It's too funny," she said. "I was talking to Captain Biggar about it last night, and I told him one of my husbands gave it to me, but I couldn't remember which. It was Mr. Spottsworth, of course. So silly of me to have forgotten."

Bill gulped.

"Are you sure?"

"Oh, quite."

"It . . . it wasn't given to you by some fellow on one of those hunting expeditions . . . as a . . . as a sort of memento?"

Mrs. Spottsworth stared.

"What *do* you mean?"

"Well, I thought . . . fellow grateful for kindnesses . . . saying good-bye . . . might have said 'Won't you accept this as a little memento . . . and all that sort of thing'."

The suggestion plainly offended Mrs. Spottsworth.

"Do you imagine that I accept diamond pendants from 'fellows', as you call them?"

"Well, I——"

"I wouldn't dream of such a thing. Mr. Spottsworth bought that pendant when we were in Bombay. I can remember it as if it were yesterday. A funny little shop with a very fat Chinaman behind the counter, and Mr. Spottsworth would insist on trying to speak Chinese. And just as he was bargaining, there was an earthquake. Not a bad one, but everything was all red dust for about ten minutes, and when it cleared, Mr. Spottsworth said 'Let's get out of here!' and paid what the man was asking and grabbed the pendant and we raced out and never stopped running till we had got back to the hotel."

A dull despair had Bill in its grip. He heaved himself painfully to his feet.

"I wonder if you would excuse me," he said. "I have to see Jeeves about something."

"Well, ring for Jeeves."

Bill shook his head.

"No, I think, if you don't mind, I'll go and see him in his pantry."

It had occurred to him that in Jeeves's pantry there would be a drop of port, and a drop of port or some similar restorative was what his stricken soul craved.

18

WHEN Rory and Monica entered Jeeves's pantry, they found its proprietor reading a letter. His fine face, always grave, seemed a little graver than usual, as if the letter's contents had disturbed him.

"Sorry to interrupt you, Jeeves," said Monica.

"Not at all, m'lady."

"Finish your reading."

"I had already done so, m'lady. A communication from Mr. Wooster."

"Oh?" said Rory. "Bertie Wooster, eh? How is the old bounder? Robust?"

"Mr. Wooster says nothing to indicate the contrary, sir."

"Good. Rosy cheeks, eh? Eating his spinach, no doubt? Capital. Couldn't be better. Still, be that as it may," said Rory, "what do you think of Taj Mahal for this afternoon's beano at Epsom Downs? I thought of slapping my two quid on its nose, with your approval."

"And Moke the Second," said Monica. "That's my fancy."

Jeeves considered.

"I see no objection to a small wager on the animal you have named sir, nor on yours, m'lady. One must bear in mind, however, that the Derby is always an extremely open race."

"Don't I know it!"

"It would be advisable, therefore, if the funds are sufficient, to endeavour to save your stake by means of a bet each way on some other horse."

"Rory thought of Escalator. I'm hesitating."

Jeeves coughed.

"Has your ladyship considered the Irish horse, Ballymore?"

"Oh, Jeeves, for heaven's sake. None of the nibs even mention it. No, not Ballymore, Jeeves. I'll have to think of something."

"Very good, m'lady. Would there be anything further?"

"Yes," said Rory. "Now that we're all here together, cheek by jowl as it were, a word from our sponsor on a personal matter,

Jeeves. What was all that that Mrs. Dogsbody was saying at lunch about you and her being out on the tiles last night?"

"Sir?"

"Weren't you in the room when she was talking about it?"

"No, m'lady."

"She said you bowled off together in the small hours to the ruined chapel."

"Ah, yes, m'lady. I apprehend Sir Roderick's meaning now. Mrs. Spottsworth did desire me to escort her to the ruined chapel last night. She was hoping to see the wraith of Lady Agatha, she informed me."

"Any luck?"

"No, m'lady."

"She says Bill saw the old girl."

"Yes, m'lady."

Rory uttered the gratified exclamation of one who has solved a mystery.

"So that's why Bill's looking like a piece of cheese today. It must have scared him stiff."

"I believe Lord Rowcester was somewhat moved by the experience, Sir Roderick. But I fancy that if, as you say, there is a resemblance between his lordship and a portion of cheese, it is occasioned more by the circumstance of his lordship's matrimonial plans having been cancelled than by any manifestation from the spirit world."

Monica squeaked excitedly.

"You don't mean Bill's engagement is off?"

"That is what I was endeavouring to convey, m'lady. Miss Wyvern handed me the ring in person, to return to his lordship. 'Am I to infer, miss,' I ventured to inquire, 'that there is a symbolical significance attached to this gesture?' and Miss Wyvern replied in the affirmative."

"Well, I'll be blowed. Poor old Bill!"

"Yes, m'lady."

"The heart bleeds."

"Yes, Sir Roderick."

It was at this moment that Bill came charging in. Seeing his sister and her husband, he stopped.

"Oh, hullo, Rory," he said. "Hullo, Moke. I'd forgotten you were here."

Rory advanced with outstretched hand. The dullest eye could

have seen that he was registering compassion. He clasped Bill's right hand in his own, and with his left hand kneaded Bill's shoulder. A man, he knew, wants sympathy at a time like this. It is in such a crisis in his affairs that he thanks heaven that he has an understanding brother-in-law, a brother-in-law who knows how to give a pep talk.

"We are not only here, old man," he said, "but we have just heard from Jeeves a bit of news that has frozen our blood. He says the girl Jill has returned you to store. Correct? I see it is. Too bad, too bad. But don't let it get you down, boy. You must . . . how would you put it, Jeeves?"

"Stiffen the sinews, summon up the blood, Sir Roderick."

"Precisely. You want to take the big, broad, spacious view, Bill. You are a fiancée short, let's face it, and your immediate reaction is, no doubt, a disposition to rend the garments and scatter ashes on the head. But you've got to look at these things from every angle, Bill, old man. Remember what Shakespeare said: 'A woman is only a woman, but a good cigar is a smoke.'"

Jeeves winced.

"Kipling, Sir Roderick."

"And here's another profound truth. I don't know who said this one. All cats are grey in the dark."

Monica spoke. Her lips, as she listened, had been compressed. There was a strange light in her eyes.

"Splendid. Go on."

Rory stopped kneading Bill's shoulder and patted it.

"At the moment," he resumed, "you are reeling from the shock, and very naturally, too. You feel you've lost something valuable, and of course I suppose one might say you have, for Jill's a nice enough kid, no disputing that. But don't be too depressed about it. Look for the silver lining, whenever clouds appear in the blue, as I have frequently sung in my bath and you, I imagine, in yours. Don't forget you're back in circulation again. Personally, I think it's an extremely nice slice of luck for you that this has happened. A bachelor's life is the only happy one, old man. When it comes to love, there's a lot to be said for the 'à la carte' as opposed to the 'table d'hôte'."

"Jeeves," said Monica.

"M'lady?"

"What was the name of the woman who drove a spike into her husband's head? It's in the Bible somewhere."

"I fancy your ladyship is thinking of the story of Jael. But she and the gentleman into whose head she drove the spike were not married, merely good friends."

"Still, her ideas were basically sound."

"It was generally considered so in her circle of acquaintance, m'lady."

"Have you a medium-sized spike, Jeeves? No? I must look in at the ironmonger's," said Monica. "Good-bye, Table d'hôte."

She walked out, and Rory watched her go, concerned. His was not a very quick mind, but he seemed to sense something wrong.

"I say! She's miffed. Eh, Jeeves?"

"I received that impression, Sir Roderick."

"Dash it all, I was only saying that stuff about marriage to cheer you up, Bill. Jeeves, where can I get some flowers? And don't say 'At the flower shop', because I simply can't sweat all the way to the town. Would there be flowers in the garden?"

"In some profusion, Sir Roderick."

"I'll go and pluck her a bouquet. That's a thing you'll find it useful to remember, Bill, if ever you get married, not that you're likely to, of course, the way things are shaping. Always remember that when the gentler sex get miffed, flowers will bring them round every time."

The door closed. Jeeves turned to Bill.

"Your lordship wished to see me about something?" he said courteously.

Bill passed a hand over his throbbing brow.

"Jeeves," he said, "I hardly know how to begin. Have you an aspirin about you?"

"Certainly, m'lord. I have just been taking one myself."

He produced a small tin box, and held it out.

"Thank you, Jeeves. Don't slam the lid."

"No, m'lord."

"And now," said Bill, "to tell you all."

Jeeves listened with gratifyingly close attention while he poured out his tale. There was no need for Bill at its conclusion to ask him if he had got the gist. It was plain from the gravity of his 'Most disturbing, m'lord' that he had got it nicely. Jeeves always got gists.

"If ever a man was in the soup," said Bill, summing up, "I am. I have been played up and made a sucker of. What are those things people get used as, Jeeves?"

"Cat's-paws, m'lord?"

"That's right. Cat's-paws. This blighted Biggar has used me as a cat's-paw. He told me the tale. Like an ass, I believed him. I pinched the pendant, swallowing that whole story of his about it practically belonging to him and he only wanted to borrow it for a few hours, and off he went to London with it, and I don't suppose we shall ever seen him again. Do you?"

"It would appear improbable, m'lord."

"One of those remote contingencies, what?"

"Extremely remote, I fear, m'lord."

"You wouldn't care to kick me, Jeeves?"

"No, m'lord."

"I've been trying to kick myself, but it's so dashed difficult if you aren't a contortionist. All that stuff about stingahs and long bars and the chap Sycamore! We ought to have seen through it in an instant."

"We ought, indeed, m'lord."

"I suppose that when a man has a face as red as that, one tends to feel that he must be telling the truth."

"Very possibly, m'lord."

"And his eyes were so bright and blue. Well, there it is," said Bill. "Whether it was the red face or the blue eyes that did it, one cannot say, but the fact remains that as a result of the general colour scheme I allowed myself to be used as a cat's-paw and pinched an expensive pendant which the hellhound Biggar has gone off to London with, thus rendering myself liable to an extended sojourn in the cooler . . . unless——"

"M'lord?"

"I was going to say 'Unless you have something to suggest'. Silly of me," said Bill, with a hollow laugh. "How could you possibly have anything to suggest?"

"I have, m'lord."

Bill stared.

"You wouldn't try to be funny at a time like this, Jeeves?"

"Certainly not, m'lord."

"You really have a life-belt to throw me before the gumbo closes over my head?"

"Yes, m'lord. In the first place, I would point out to your lordship that there is little or no likelihood of your lordship becoming suspect of the theft of Mrs. Spottsworth's ornament. It has disappeared. Captain Biggar has disappeared. The authorities will put two and two together, m'lord, and automatically credit him with the crime."

"Something in that."

"It would seem impossible, m'lord, for them to fall into any other train of thought."

Bill brightened a little, but only a little.

"Well, that's all to the good, I agree, but it doesn't let me out. You've overlooked something, Jeeves."

"M'lord?"

"The honour of the Rowcesters. That is the snag we come up against. I can't go through life feeling that under my own roof—leaky, but still a roof—I have swiped a valuable pendant from a guest filled to the eyebrows with my salt. How am I to reimburse La Spottsworth? That is the problem to which we have to bend our brains."

"I was about to touch on that point, m'lord. Your lordship will recall that in speaking of suspicion falling upon Captain Biggar I said 'In the first place'. In the second place, I was about to add, restitution can readily be made to Mrs. Spottsworth, possibly in the form of notes to the correct amount dispatched anonymously to her address, if the lady can be persuaded to purchase Rowcester Abbey."

"Great Scott, Jeeves!"

"M'lord?"

"The reason I used the expression 'Great Scott!' " said Bill, his emotion still causing him to quiver from head to foot, "was that in the rush and swirl of recent events I had absolutely forgotten all about selling the house. Of course! That would fix up everything, wouldn't it?"

"Unquestionably, m'lord. Even a sale at a sacrifice price would enable your lordship to do——"

"The square thing?"

"Precisely, m'lord. I may add that while on our way to the ruined chapel last night, Mrs. Spottsworth spoke in high terms of the charms of Rowcester Abbey and was equally cordial in her remarks as we were returning. All in all, m'lord, I would say that the prospects were distinctly favourable, and if I might offer the suggestion, I think that your lordship should now withdraw to the library and obtain material for what is termed a sales talk by skimming through the advertisements in *Country Life*, in which, as your lordship is possibly aware, virtually every large house which has been refused as a gift by the National Trust is offered for sale. The language is extremely persuasive."

"Yes, I know the sort of thing. 'This lordly demesne, with its avenues of historic oaks, its tumbling streams alive with trout and tench, its breath-taking vistas lined with flowering shrubs . . . ' Yes, I'll bone up."

"It might possibly assist your lordship if I were to bring a small bottle of champagne to the library."

"You think of everything, Jeeves."

"Your lordship is too kind."

"Half a bot should do the trick."

"I think so, m'lord, if adequately iced."

It was some minutes later, as Jeeves was passing through the living-room with the brain-restorer on a small tray, that Jill came in through the French window.

19

I T is a characteristic of women as a sex, and one that does credit
to their gentle hearts, that—unless they are gangster's molls or
something of that kind—they shrink from the thought of violence.
Even when love is dead, they dislike the idea of the man to whom
they were once betrothed receiving a series of juicy ones from a
horsewhip in the competent hands of an elderly, but still muscular,
Chief Constable of a county. When they hear such a Chief Constable sketching out plans for an operation of this nature, their
instinct is to hurry to the prospective victim's residence and warn
him of his peril by outlining the shape of things to come.

It was to apprise Bill of her father's hopes and dreams that Jill
had come to Rowcester Abbey and, not being on speaking terms
with her former fiancé, she had been wondering a little how the
information she was bringing could be conveyed to him. The sight
of Jeeves cleared up this point. A few words of explanation to
Jeeves, coupled with the suggestion that he should advise Bill to
lie low till the old gentleman had blown over, would accomplish
what she had in mind, and she could then go home again, her duty
done and the whole unpleasant affair disposed of.

"Oh, Jeeves," she said.

Jeeves had turned, and was regarding her with respectful bene-
volence.

"Good afternoon, miss. You will find his lordship in the library."

Jill stiffened haughtily. There was not much of her, but what
there was she drew to its full height.

"No, I won't," she replied in a voice straight from the frigidaire,
"because I'm jolly well not going there. I haven't the slightest wish
to speak to Lord Rowcester. I want you to give him a message."

"Very good, miss."

"Tell him my father is coming here to borrow his horsewhip to
horsewhip him with."

"Miss?"

"It's quite simple, isn't it? You know my father?"

"Yes, miss."

"And you know what a horsewhip is?"

"Yes, miss."

"Well, tell Lord Rowcester the combination is on its way over."

"And if his lordship should express curiosity as to the reason for Colonel Wyvern's annoyance?"

"You may say it's because I told him about what happened last night. Or this morning, to be absolutely accurate. At two o'clock this morning. He'll understand."

"At two o'clock this morning, miss? That would have been at about the hour when I was escorting Mrs. Spottsworth to the ruined chapel. The lady had expressed a wish to establish contact with the apparition of Lady Agatha. The wife of Sir Caradoc the Crusader, miss, who did well, I believe, at the Battle of Joppa. She is reputed to haunt the ruined chapel."

Jill collapsed into a chair. A sudden wild hope, surging through the cracks in her broken heart, had shaken her from stem to stern, making her feel boneless.

"What . . . what did you say?"

Jeeves was a kindly man, and not only a kindly man but a man who could open a bottle of champagne as quick as a flash. It was in something of the spirit of the Sir Philip Sidney who gave the water to the stretcher case that he now whisked the cork from the bottle he was carrying. Jill's need, he felt, was greater than Bill's.

"Permit me, miss."

Jill drank gratefully. Her eyes had widened, and the colour was returning to her face.

"Jeeves, this is a matter of life and death," she said. "At two o'clock this morning I saw Lord Rowcester coming out of Mrs. Spottsworth's room looking perfectly frightful in mauve pyjamas. Are you telling me that Mrs. Spottsworth was not there?"

"Precisely, miss. She was with me in the ruined chapel, holding me spellbound with her account of recent investigations of the Society of Psychical Research."

"Then what was Lord Rowcester doing in her room?"

"Purloining the lady's pendant, miss."

It was unfortunate that as he said these words Jill should have been taking a sip of champagne, for she choked. And as her companion would have considered it a liberty to slap her on the back, it was some moments before she was able to speak.

"Purloining Mrs. Spottsworth's pendant?"

"Yes, miss. It is a long and somewhat intricate story, but if you would care for me to run through the salient points, I should be delighted to do so. Would it interest you to hear the inside history of his lordship's recent activities, culminating, as I have indicated, in the abstracting of Mrs. Spottsworth's ornament?"

Jill drew in her breath with a hiss.

"Yes, Jeeves, it would."

"Very good, miss. Then must I speak of one who loved not wisely but too well, of one whose subdued eyes, albeit unused to the melting mood, drop tears as fast as the Arabian trees their medicinal gum."

"Jeeves!"

"Miss?"

"What on earth are you talking about?"

Jeeves looked a little hurt.

"I was endeavouring to explain that it was for love of you, miss, that his lordship became a Silver Ring bookmaker."

"A *what?*"

"Having plighted his troth to you, miss, his lordship felt—rightly, in my opinion—that in order to support a wife he would require a considerably larger income than he had been enjoying up to that moment. After weighing and rejecting the claims of other professions, he decided to embark on the career of a bookmaker in the Silver Ring, trading under the name of Honest Patch Perkins. I officiated as his lordship's clerk. We wore false moustaches."

Jill opened her mouth, then, as if feeling that any form of speech would be inadequate, closed it again.

"For a time the venture paid very handsomely. In three days at Doncaster we were so fortunate as to amass no less a sum than four hundred and twenty pounds, and it was in optimistic mood that we proceeded to Epsom for the Oaks. But disaster was lurking in wait for his lordship. To use the metaphor that the tide turned would be inaccurate. What smote his lordship was not so much the tide as a single tidal wave. Captain Biggar, miss. He won a double at his lordship's expense—five pounds on Lucy Glitters at a hundred to six, all to come on Whistler's Mother, S.P."

Jill spoke faintly.

"What was the S.P.?"

"I deeply regret to say, miss, thirty-three to one. And as he had rashly refused to lay the wager off, this cataclysm left his lordship in the unfortunate position of owing Captain Biggar in excess of three thousand pounds, with no assets with which to meet his obligations."

"Golly!"

"Yes, miss. His lordship was compelled to make a somewhat hurried departure from the course, followed by Captain Biggar, shouting 'Welsher!', but when we were able to shake off our pursuer's challenge some ten miles from the Abbey, we were hoping that the episode was concluded and that to Captain Biggar his lordship would remain merely a vague, unidentified figure in a moustache by Clarkson. But it was not to be, miss. The Captain tracked his lordship here, penetrated his incognito and demanded an immediate settlement."

"But Bill had no money."

"Precisely, miss. His lordship did not omit to stress that point. And it was then that Captain Biggar proposed that his lordship should secure possession of Mrs. Spottsworth's pendant, asserting, when met with a *nolle prosequi* on his lordship's part, that the object in question had been given by him to the lady some years ago, so that he was morally entitled to borrow it. The story, on reflection, seems somewhat thin, but it was told with so great a wealth of corroborative detail that it convinced us at the time, and his lordship, who had been vowing that he would ne'er consent, consented. Do I make myself clear, miss?"

"Quite clear. You don't mind my head swimming?"

"Not at all, miss. The question then arose of how the operation was to be carried through, and eventually it was arranged that I should lure Mrs. Spottsworth from her room on the pretext that Lady Agatha had been seen in the ruined chapel, and during her absence his lordship should enter and obtain the trinket. This ruse proved successful. The pendant was duly handed to Captain Biggar, who has taken it to London with the purpose of pawning it and investing the proceeds on the Irish horse, Ballymore, concerning whose chances he is extremely sanguine. As regards his lordship's mauve pyjamas, to which you made a derogatory allusion a short while back, I am hoping to convince his lordship that a quiet blue or a pistachio green——"

But Jill was not interested in the Rowcester pyjamas and the steps which were being taken to correct their mauveness. She was hammering on the library door.

"Bill! Bill!" she cried, like a woman wailing for her demon lover, and Bill, hearing that voice, came out with the promptitude of a cork extracted by Jeeves from a bottle.

"Oh, Bill!" said Jill, flinging herself into his arms. "Jeeves has told me everything!"

Over the head that rested on his chest Bill shot an anxious glance at Jeeves.

"When you say everything, do you mean *everything?*"

"Yes, m'lord. I deemed it advisable."

"I know all about Honest Patch Perkins and your moustache and Captain Biggar and Whistler's Mother and Mrs. Spottsworth and the pendant," said Jill, nestling closely.

It seemed so odd to Bill that a girl who knew all this should be nestling closely that he was obliged to release her for a moment and step across and take a sip of champagne.

"And you really mean," he said, returning and folding her in his embrace once more, "that you don't recoil from me in horror?"

"Of course I don't recoil from you in horror. Do I look as if I were recoiling from you in horror?"

"Well, no," said Bill, having considered this. He kissed her lips, her forehead, her ears and the top of her head. "But the trouble is that you might just as well recoil from me in horror, because I don't see how the dickens we're ever going to get married. I haven't a bean, and I've somehow got to raise a small fortune to pay Mrs. Spottsworth for her pendant. *Noblesse oblige*, if you follow my drift. So if I don't sell her the house——"

"Of course you'll sell her the house."

"Shall I? I wonder—I'll certainly try. Where on earth's she disappeared to? She was in here when I came through into the library just now. I wish she'd show up. I'm all full of that *Country Life* stuff, and if she doesn't come soon, it will evaporate."

"Excuse me, m'lord," said Jeeves, who during the recent exchanges had withdrawn discreetly to the window. "Mrs. Spottsworth and her ladyship are at this moment crossing the lawn."

With a courteous gesture he stepped to one side, and Mrs. Spottsworth entered, followed by Monica.

"Jill!" cried Monica, halting, amazed. "Good heavens!"

"Oh, it's all right," said Jill. "There's been a change in the situation. Sweethearts still."

"Well, that's fine. I've been showing Rosalinda round the place——"

"——with its avenues of historic oaks, its tumbling streams alive with trout and tench, and its breath-taking vistas lined with flowering shrubs . . . How did you like it?" said Bill.

Mrs. Spottsworth clasped her hands and closed her eyes in an ecstasy.

"It's wonderful, wonderful!" she said. "I can't understand how you can bring yourself to part with it, Billiken."

Bill gulped. "Am I going to part with it?"

"You certainly are," said Mrs. Spottsworth emphatically, "if I have anything to say about it. This is the house of my dreams. How much do you want for it—lock, stock and barrel?"

"You've taken my breath away."

"Well, that's me. I never could endure beating about the bush. If I want a thing, I say so and write a note. I'll tell you what let's do. Suppose I pay you a deposit of two thousand, and we can decide on the purchase price later?"

"You couldn't make it three thousand?"

"Sure." Mrs. Spottsworth unscrewed her fountain pen and having unscrewed it, paused. "There's just one thing, though, before I sign on the dotted line. This place isn't damp, is it?"

"*Damp?*" said Monica. "Why, of course not."

"You're sure?"

"Dry as a bone."

"That's swell. Damp is death to me. Fibrositis *and* sciatica."

Rory came in through the French window, laden with roses.

"A nosegay for you, Moke, old girl, with comps. of R. Carmoyle," he said, pressing the blooms into Monica's hands. "I say, Bill, it's starting to rain."

"What of it?"

"What *of* it?" echoed Rory, surprised. "My dear old boy, you know what happens in this house when it rains. Water through the roof, water through the walls, water, water everywhere. I was merely about to suggest in a kindly Boy Scout sort of spirit that you had better put buckets under the upstairs skylight. Very damp house, this," he said, addressing Mrs. Spottsworth in his genial, confidential way. "So near the river, you know. I often say that whereas in the summer months the river is at the bottom of the garden, in the winter months the garden is at the bottom of the——"

"Excuse me, m'lady," said the housemaid Ellen, appearing in the doorway. "Could I speak to Mrs. Spottsworth, m'lady?"

Mrs. Spottsworth, who had been staring, aghast, at Rory, turned, pen in hand.

"Yes?"

"Moddom," said Ellen, "your pendant's been pinched."

She had never been a girl for breaking things gently.

⋆ 20 ⋆

WITH considerable gratification Ellen found herself the centre of attraction. All eyes were focused upon her, and most of them were bulging. Bill's, in particular, struck her as being on the point of leaving their sockets.

"Yes," she proceeded, far too refined to employ the Bulstrode-Trelawny 'Yus', "I was laying out your clothes for the evening, moddom, and I said to myself that you'd probably be wishing to wear the pendant again tonight, so I ventured to look in the little box, and it wasn't there, moddom. It's been stolen."

Mrs. Spottsworth drew a quick breath. The trinket in question was of little intrinsic worth—it could not, as she had said to Captain Biggar, have cost more than ten thousand dollars—but, as she had also said to Captain Biggar, it had a sentimental value for her. She was about to express her concern in words, but Bill broke in.

"What do you mean, it's been stolen?" he demanded hotly. You could see that the suggestion outraged him. "You probably didn't look properly."

Ellen was respectful, but firm.

"It's gone, m'lord."

"You may have dropped it somewhere, Mrs. Spottsworth," said Jill. "Was the clasp loose?"

"Why, yes," said Mrs. Spottsworth. "The clasp was loose. But I distinctly remember putting it in its case last night."

"Not there now, moddom," said Ellen, rubbing it in.

"Let's go up and have a thorough search," said Monica.

"We will," said Mrs. Spottsworth. "But I'm afraid . . . very much afraid——"

She followed Ellen out of the room. Monica, pausing at the door, eyed Rory balefully for an instant.

"Well, Bill," she said, "so you don't sell the house, after all. And if Big Mouth there hadn't come barging in prattling about water and buckets, that cheque would have been signed."

She swept out, and Rory looked at Bill, surprised.

"I say, did I drop a brick?"

Bill laughed hackingly.

"If one followed you about for a month, one would have enough bricks to build a house."

"In *re* this pendant. Anything I can do?"

"Yes, keep out of it."

"I could nip off in the car and fetch some of the local constabulary."

"Keep right out of it." Bill looked at his watch. "The Derby will be starting in a few minutes. Go in there and get the television working."

"Right," said Rory. "But if I'm needed, give me a shout."

He disappeared into the library, and Bill turned to Jeeves, who had once again effaced himself. In times of domestic crisis, Jeeves had the gift, possessed by all good butlers, of creating the illusion that he was not there. He was standing now at the extreme end of the room, looking stuffed.

"Jeeves!"

"M'lord?" said Jeeves, coming to life like a male Galatea.

"Any suggestions?"

"None of practical value, m'lord. But a thought has just occurred which enables me to take a somewhat brighter view of the situation. We were speaking not long since of Captain Biggar as a gentleman who had removed himself permanently from our midst. Does it not seem likely to your lordship that in the event of Ballymore emerging victorious the Captain, finding himself in possession of ample funds, will carry out his original plan of redeeming the pendant, bringing it back and affecting to discover it on the premises?"

Bill chewed his lip.

"You think so?"

"It would be the prudent course for him to pursue, m'lord. Suspicion, as I say, must inevitably rest upon him, and failure to return the ornament would place him in the disagreeable position of becoming a hunted man in hourly danger of being apprehended by the authorities. I am convinced that if Ballymore wins, we shall see Captain Biggar again."

"*If* Ballymore wins."

"Precisely, m'lord."

"Then one's whole future hangs on whether it does."

"That is how matters stand, m'lord."

Jill uttered a passionate cry.

"I'm going to start praying!"

"Yes, do," said Bill. "Pray that Ballymore will run as he has never run before. Pray like billy-o. Pray all over the house. Pray——"

Monica and Mrs. Spottsworth came back.

"Well," said Monica, "it's gone. There's no doubt about that. I've just phoned for the police."

Bill reeled.

"What!"

"Yes. Rosalinda didn't want me to, but I insisted. I told her you wouldn't dream of not doing everything you could to catch the thief."

"You . . . You think the thing's been stolen?"

"It's the only possible explanation."

Mrs. Spottsworth sighed.

"Oh, dear! I really am sorry to have started all this trouble."

"Nonsense, Rosalinda. Bill doesn't mind. All Bill wants is to see the crook caught and bunged into the cooler. Isn't it, Bill?"

"Yes, *sir!*" said Bill.

"For a good long stretch, too, let's hope."

"We mustn't be vindictive."

"No," said Mrs. Spottsworth. "You're quite right. Justice, but not vengeance."

"Well, one thing's certain," said Monica. "It's an inside job."

Bill stirred uneasily.

"Oh, do you think so?"

"Yes, and I've got a pretty shrewd idea who the guilty party is."

"Who?"

"Someone who was in a terrible state of nerves this morning."

"Oh?"

"His cup and saucer were rattling like castanets."

"When was this?"

"At breakfast. Do you want me to name names?"

"Go ahead."

"Captain Biggar!"

Mrs. Spottsworth started.

"What!"

"You weren't down, Rosalinda, or I'm sure you would have noticed it, too. He was as nervous as a treeful of elephants."

"Oh, no, no! Captain Biggar? That I can't and won't believe. If Captain Biggar were guilty, I should lose my faith in human nature. And that would be a far worse blow than losing the pendant."

"The pendant is gone, and he's gone. It adds up, don't you think? Oh, well," said Monica, "we shall soon know."

"What makes you so sure of that?"

"Why, the jewel-case, of course. The police will take it away and test it for fingerprints. What on earth's the matter, Bill?"

"Nothing's the matter," said Bill, who had leaped some eighteen inches into the air but saw no reason for revealing the sudden agonized thought which had motivated this adagio exhibition. "Er, Jeeves."

"M'lord?"

"Lady Carmoyle is speaking of Mrs. Spottsworth's jewel-case."

"Yes, m'lord?"

"She threw out the interesting suggestion that the miscreant might have forgotten to wear gloves, in which event the bally thing would be covered with his fingerprints. That would be lucky, wouldn't it?"

"Extremely fortunate, m'lord."

"I'll bet he's wishing he hadn't been such an ass."

"Yes, m'lord."

"And that he could wipe them off."

"Yes, m'lord."

"You might go and get the thing, so as to have it ready for the police when they arrive."

"Very good, m'lord."

"Hold it by the edges, Jeeves. You don't want to disturb those fingerprints."

"I will exercise the greatest care, m'lord," said Jeeves, and went out, and almost simultaneously Colonel Wyvern came in through the French window.

At the moment of his entry Jill, knowing that when a man is in a state of extreme agitation there is nothing he needs more than a woman's gentle sympathy, had put her arms round Bill's neck and was kissing him tenderly. The spectacle brought the Colonel to a halt. It confused him. With this sort of thing going on, it was difficult to lead up to the subject of horsewhips.

"Ha, hrr'mph!" he said, and Monica spun round, astounded.

"My goodness!" she said. "You have been quick. It's only five minutes since I phoned."

"Eh?"

"Hullo, father," said Jill. "We were just waiting for you to show up. Have you brought your bloodhounds and magnifying glass?"

"What the dickens are you talking about?"

Monica was perplexed.

"Didn't you come in answer to my phone call, Colonel?"

"You keep talking about a phone call. What phone call? I came to see Lord Rowcester on a personal matter. What's all this about a phone call?"

"Mrs. Spottsworth's diamond pendant has been stolen, father."

"What? What? What?"

"This is Mrs. Spottsworth," said Monica. "Colonel Wyvern, Rosalinda, our Chief Constable."

"Charmed," said Colonel Wyvern, bowing gallantly, but an instant later he was the keen, remorseless police officer again. "Had your pendant stolen, eh? Bad show, bad show." He took out a note-book and a pencil. "An inside job, was it?"

"That's what we think."

"Then I'll have to have a list of everybody in the house."

Jill stepped forward, her hands extended.

"Wyvern, Jill," she said. "Slip on the bracelets, officer. I'll come quietly."

"Oh, don't be an ass," said Colonel Wyvern.

Something struck the door gently. It might have been a foot. Bill opened the door, revealing Jeeves. He was carrying the jewel-case, a handkerchief at its extreme edges.

"Thank you, m'lord," he said.

He advanced to the table and lowered the case on to it very carefully.

"Here is the case the pendant was in," said Mrs. Spottsworth.

"Good." Colonel Wyvern eyed Jeeves with approval. "Glad to see you were careful about handling it, my man."

"Oh, trust Jeeves for that," said Bill.

"And now," said Colonel Wyvern, "for the names."

As he spoke, the library door burst open, and Rory came dashing out, horror written on his every feature.

I SAY, chaps," said Rory, "the most appalling thing has happened!"

Monica moaned.

"Not something *more?*"

"This is the absolute frozen limit. The Derby is just starting——"

"Rory, the Chief Constable is here."

"—and the television set has gone on the blink. Oh, it's my fault, I suppose. I was trying to get a perfect adjustment, and I must have twiddled the wrong thingummy."

"Rory, this is Colonel Wyvern, the Chief Constable."

"How are you, Chief C.? Do you know anything about television?"

The Colonel drew himself up.

"I do not!"

"You couldn't fix a set?" said Rory wistfully. "Not that there's time, of course. The race will be over. What about the radio?"

"In the corner, Sir Roderick," said Jeeves.

"Oh, thank Heaven!" cried Rory, galloping to it. "Come on and give me a hand, Jeeves."

The Chief Constable spoke coldly.

"Who is this gentleman?"

"Such as he is," said Monica apologetically, "my husband, Sir Roderick Carmoyle."

Colonel Wyvern advanced on Rory as majestically as his lack of inches permitted, and addressed the seat of his trousers, the only portion of him visible as he bent over the radio.

"Sir Roderick, I am conducting an investigation."

"But you'll hold it up to listen to the Derby?"

"When on duty, Sir Roderick, I allow nothing to interfere. I want a list——"

The radio, suddenly blaring forth, gave him one.

". . . Taj Mahal, Sweet William, Garniture, Moke the Second, Voleur . . . Quite an impressive list, isn't it?" said the radio. There goes Gordon Richards. Lots of people think this will be his lucky day. I don't see Bellwether . . . Oh, yes, he's turning round now and walking back to the gate . . . They should be off in just a moment . . . Sorry, no. Two more have turned round. One of them is being *very* temperamental. It looks like Simple Simon. No, it's the Irish outsider, Ballymore."

The Chief Constable frowned. "Really, I must ask——"

"Okay. I'll turn it down," said Rory, and immediately, being Rory, turned it up.

"They're in line now," yelled the radio, like a costermonger calling attention to his blood oranges, "all twenty-six of them . . . They're OFF . . . Ballymore is left at the post."

Jill screamed shrilly. "Oh, *no!*"

"Vaurien," proceeded the radio, now, owing to Rory's ministrations, speaking in an almost inaudible whisper, like an invalid uttering a few last words from a sick-bed, "is in front, the Boussac pacemaker." Its voice strengthened a little. "Taj Mahal is just behind. I see Escalator. Escalator's going very strong. I see Sweet William. I see Moke the Second. I see . . ." Here the wasting sickness set in again, and the rest was lost in a sort of mouselike squeak.

The Chief Constable drew a relieved breath.

"Ha! At last! Now then, Lord Rowcester. What servants have you here?"

Bill did not answer. Like a mechanical figure he was moving toward the radio, as if drawn by some invisible force.

"There's a cook," said Monica.

"A widow, sir," said Jeeves. "Mary Jane Piggott."

Rory looked round.

"Piggott? Who said Piggott?"

"A housemaid," said Monica, as Jill, like Bill, was drawn toward the radio as if in a trance. "Her name's Ellen. Ellen what, Jeeves?"

"French, m'lady. Ellen Tallulah French."

"The French horse," bellowed the radio, suddenly acquiring a new access of strength, "is still in front, then Moke the Second, Escalator, Taj Mahal . . ."

"What about the gardener?"

"No, not Gardener," said Rory. "You mean Garniture."

". . . Sweet William, Oratory . . . Vaurien's falling back, and Garniture——"

"You see?" said Rory.

"—and Moke the Second moving up."

"That's mine," said Monica, and with a strange, set look on her face began to move toward the radio.

"Looks quite as though Gordon Richards might be going to win the Derby at last. They're down the hill and turning Tattenham Corner, Moke the Second in front, with Gordon up. Only three and a half furlongs to go . . ."

"Yes, sir," said Jeeves, completely unmoved, "there is a gardener, an old man named Percy Wellbeloved."

The radio suddenly broke into a frenzy of excitement.

"Oo! . . . Oo! . . . There's a horse coming up on the outside. It's coming like an express train. I can't identify . . ."

"Gee, this is exciting, isn't it!" said Mrs. Spottsworth.

She went to the radio. Jeeves alone remained at the Chief Constable's side. Colonel Wyvern was writing laboriously in his notebook.

"It's Ballymore. The horse on the outside is Ballymore. He's challenging the Moke. Hear that crowd roaring 'Come on, Gordon!'."

"Moke . . . The Moke . . . Gordon," wrote Colonel Wyvern.

"Come on, Gordon!" shouted Monica.

The radio was now becoming incoherent.

"It's Ballymore . . . No, it's the Moke . . . No, Ballymore . . . No, the Moke . . . No . . ."

"Make up your mind," advised Rory.

For some moments Colonel Wyvern had been standing motionless, his note-book frozen in his hand. Now a sort of shudder passed through him, and his eyes grew wide and wild. Brandishing his pencil, he leaped toward the radio.

"Come on, Gordon!" he roared. "COME ON, GORDON!!!"

"Come on, Ballymore," said Jeeves with quiet dignity.

The radio had now given up all thoughts of gentlemanly restraint. It was as though on honeydew it had fed and drunk the milk of Paradise.

"Photo finish!" it shrieked. "Photo finish! Photo finish! First time in the history of the Derby. Photo finish. Escalator in third place."

Rather sheepishly the Chief Constable turned away and came back to Jeeves.

"The gardener's name you said was what? Clarence Wilberforce, was it?"

"Percy Wellbeloved, sir."

"Odd name."

"Shropshire, I believe, sir."

"Ah? Percy Wellbeloved. Does that complete the roster of the staff?"

"Yes, sir, except for myself."

Rory came away from the radio, mopping his forehead.

"Well, that Taj Mahal let me down with a bang," he said bitterly. "Why is it one can never pick a winner in this bally race?"

" 'The Moke' didn't suggest a winner to you?" said Monica.

"Eh? No. Why? Why should it?"

"God bless you, Roderick Carmoyle."

Colonel Wyvern was himself again now.

"I would like," he said, in a curt, official voice, "to inspect the scene of the robbery."

"I will take you there," said Mrs. Spottsworth. "Will you come too, Monica?"

"Yes, yes, of course," said Monica. "Listen in, some of you, will you, and see what that photo shows."

"And I'll send this down to the station," said Colonel Wyvern, picking up the jewel-case by one corner, "and find out what *it* shows."

They went out, and Rory moved to the door of the library.

"I'll go and see if I really have damaged that T.V. set," he said. "All I did was twiddle a thingummy." He stretched himself with a yawn. "Dam dull Derby," he said. "Even if Moke the Second wins, the old girl's only got ten bob on it at eights."

The library door closed behind him.

"Jeeves," said Bill, "I've got to have a drink."

"I will bring it immediately, m'lord."

"No, don't bring it. I'll come to your pantry."

"And I'll come with you," said Jill. "But we must wait to hear that result. Let's hope Ballymore had sense enough to stick out his tongue."

"Ha!" cried Bill.

The radio had begun to speak.

"Hundreds of thousands of pounds hang on what that photograph decides," it was saying in the rather subdued voice of a man recovering from a hangover. It seemed to be a little ashamed of its recent emotion. "The number should be going up at any moment. Yes, here it is . . ."

"Come on, Ballymore!" cried Jill.

"Come on, Ballymore!" shouted Bill.

"Come on, Ballymore," said Jeeves reservedly.

"Moke the Second wins," said the radio. "Hard luck on Bally-more. He ran a wonderful race. If it hadn't been for that bad start, he would have won in a canter. His defeat saves the bookies a tremendous loss. A huge sum was bet on the Irish horse ten minutes before starting time, obviously one of those S.P. jobs which are so . . ."

Dully, with something of the air of a man laying a wreath on the tomb of an old friend, Bill turned the radio off.

"Come on," he said. "After all, there's still champagne."

✱ 22 ✱

Mrs. spottsworth came slowly down the stairs. Monica and the Chief Constable were still conducting their examination of the scene of the crime, but they had been speaking freely of Captain Biggar, and the trend of their remarks had been such as to make her feel that knives were being driven through her heart. When a woman loves a man with every fibre of a generous nature, it can never be pleasant for her to hear this man alluded to as a red-faced thug (Monica) and as a scoundrel who can't possibly get away but must inevitably ere long be caught and slapped into the jug (Colonel Wyvern). It was her intention to make for that rustic seat and there sit and think of what might have been.

The rustic seat stood at a junction of two moss-grown paths facing the river which lay—though only, as we have seen, during the summer months—at the bottom of the garden. Flowering bushes masked it from the eye of one approaching, and it was not till she had turned the last corner that Mrs. Spottsworth was able to perceive that it already had an occupant. At the sight of that occupant she stood for a moment transfixed. Then there burst from her lips a cry so like that of a zebu calling to its mate that Captain Biggar, who had been sitting in a deep reverie, staring at a snail, had the momentary illusion that he was back in Africa. He sprang to his feet, and for a long instant they stood there motion-less, gazing at each other wide-eyed while the various birds, bees, wasps, gnats and other insects operating in the vicinity went about their business as if nothing at all sensational had happened. The snail, in particular, seemed completely unmoved.

Mrs. Spottsworth did not share its detached aloofness. She was stirred to her depths.

"You!" she cried. "Oh, I knew you would come. They said you wouldn't, but I knew."

Captain Biggar was hanging his head. The man seemed crushed, incapable of movement. A rhinoceros, seeing him now, would have plucked up heart and charged on him without a tremor, feeling that this was going to be easy.

170

"I couldn't do it," he muttered. "I got to thinking of you and of the chaps at the club, and I couldn't do it."

"The club?"

"The old Anglo-Malay Club in Kuala Lumpur, where men are white and honesty goes for granted. Yes, I thought of the chaps. I thought of Tubby Frobisher. Would I ever be able to look him again in that one good eye of his? And then I thought that you had trusted me because . . . because I was an Englishman. And I said to myself, it isn't only the old Anglo-Malay and Tubby and the Subahdar and Doc and Squiffy, Cuthbert Biggar—you're letting down the whole British Empire."

Mrs. Spottsworth choked.

"Did . . . did you take it?"

Captain Biggar threw up his chin and squared his shoulders. He was so nearly himself again, now that he had spoken those brave words, that the rhinoceros, taking a look at him, would have changed its mind and decided to remember an appointment elsewhere.

"I took it, and I brought it back," he said in a firm, resonant voice, producing the pendant from his hip pocket. "The idea was merely to borrow it for the day, as security for a gamble. But I couldn't do it. It might have meant a fortune, but I couldn't do it."

Mrs. Spottsworth bent her head.

"Put it round my neck, Cuthbert," she whispered.

Captain Biggar stared incredulously at her back hair.

"You want me to? You don't mind if I touch you?"

"Put it round my neck," repeated Mrs. Spottsworth.

Reverently the Captain did so, and there was a pause.

"Yes," said the Captain, "I might have made a fortune, and shall I tell you why I wanted a fortune? Don't run away with the idea that I'm a man who values money. Ask any of the chaps out East, and they'll say 'Give Bwana Biggar his .505 Gibbs, his eland steak of a night, let him breathe God's clean air and turn his face up to God's good sun and he asks nothing more'. But it was imperative that I should lay my hands on a bit of the stuff so that I might feel myself in a position to speak my love. Rosie . . . I heard them calling you that, and I must use that name . . . Rosie, I love you. I loved you from that first moment in Kenya when you stepped out of the car and I said 'Ah, the memsahib'. All these years I have dreamed of you, and on this very seat last night it was all I could do to keep myself from pouring out my heart. It doesn't matter now. I can speak now because we are parting for ever. Soon I shall be wandering out into the sunset . . . alone."

He paused, and Mrs. Spottsworth spoke. There was a certain sharpness in her voice.

"You won't be wandering out into any old sunset alone," she said. "Jiminy Christmas! What do you want to wander out into sunsets alone for?"

Captain Biggar smiled a faint, sad smile.

"I don't *want* to wander out into sunsets alone, dear lady. It's the code. The code that says a poor man must not propose marriage to a rich woman, for if he does, he loses his self-respect and ceases to play with a straight bat."

"I never heard such nonsense in my life. Who started all this apple-sauce?"

Captain Biggar stiffened a little.

"I cannot say who started it, but it is the rule that guides the lives of men like Squiffy and Doc and the Subahdah and Augustus Frobisher."

Mrs. Spottsworth uttered an exclamation.

"*Augustus* Frobisher? For Pete's sake! I've been thinking all along that there was something familiar about that name Frobisher, and now you say Augustus . . . This friend of yours, this Frobisher. Is he a fellow with a red face?"

"We all have red faces east of Suez."

"And a small, bristly moustache?"

"Small, bristly moustaches, too."

"Does he stammer slightly? Has he a small mole on the left cheek? Is one of his eyes green and the other glass?"

Captain Biggar was amazed.

"Good God! That's Tubby. You've met him?"

"Met him? You bet I've met him. It was only a week before I left the States that I was singing 'Oh, perfect love' at his wedding."

Captain Biggar's eyes widened.

"*Howki wa hoo!*" he exclaimed. "Tubby is married?"

"He certainly is. And do you know who he's married to? Cora Rita Rockmetteller, widow of the late Sigsbee Rockmetteller, the Sardine King, a woman with a darned sight more money than I've got myself. Now you see how much your old code amounts to. When Augustus Frobisher met Cora and heard that she had fifty million smackers hidden away behind the brick in the fireplace, did he wander out into any sunset alone? No, sir! He bought a clean collar and a gardenia for his buttonhole and snapped into it."

Captain Biggar had lowered himself on to the rustic seat and was breathing heavily through the nostrils.

"You have shaken me, Rosie!"

"And you needed shaking, talking all that malarkey. You and your old code!"

"I can't take it in."

"You will, if you sit and think it over for a while. You stay here and get used to the idea of walking down the aisle with me, and I'll go in and phone the papers that a marriage has been arranged and will shortly take place between Cuthbert . . . have you any other names, my precious lamb?"

"Gervase," said the Captain in a low voice. "And it's Brabazon-Biggar. With a hyphen."

". . . between Cuthbert Gervase Brabazon-Biggar and Rosa-linda Bessemer Spottsworth. It's a pity it isn't Sir Cuthbert. Say!" said Mrs. Spottsworth, struck with an idea. "What's wrong with buying you a knighthood? I wonder how much they cost these days. I'll have to ask Sir Roderick. I might be able to get it at Harrige's. Well, good-bye for the moment, my wonder man. Don't go wandering off into any sunsets."

Humming gaily, for her heart was light, Mrs. Spottsworth tripped down the moss-grown path, tripped across the lawn and tripped through the French window into the living-room. Jeeves was there. He had left Bill and Jill trying mournfully to console each other in his pantry, and had returned to the living-room to collect the coffee-cups. At the sight of the pendant encircling Mrs. Spottsworth's neck, no fewer than three hairs of his left eyebrow quivered for an instant, showing how deeply he had been moved by the spectacle.

"You're looking at the pendant, I see," said Mrs. Spottsworth, beaming happily. "I don't wonder you're surprised. Captain Biggar found it just now in the grass by that rustic seat where we were sitting last night."

It would be too much to say that Jeeves stared, but his eyes enlarged, the merest fraction, a thing they did only on special occasions.

"Has Captain Biggar returned, madam?"

"He got back a few minutes ago. Oh, Jeeves, do you know the telephone number of *The Times*?"

"No, madam, but I could ascertain."

"I want to announce my engagement to Captain Biggar."

Four hairs of Jeeves's right eyebrow stirred slightly, as if a passing breeze had disturbed them.

"Indeed, madam? May I wish you every happiness?"

"Thank you, Jeeves."

"Shall I telephone *The Times*, madam?"

"If you will, and the *Telegraph* and *Mail* and *Express*. Any others?"

"I think not, madam. Those you have mentioned should be quite sufficient for an announcement of this nature."

"Perhaps you're right. Just those, then."

"Very good, madam. Might I venture to ask, madam, if you and Captain Biggar will be taking up your residence at the Abbey?"

Mrs. Spottsworth sighed.

"No, Jeeves, I wish I could buy it . . . I love the place . . . but it's damp. This English climate!"

"Our English summers *are* severe."

"And the winters worse."

Jeeves coughed.

"I wonder if I might make a suggestion, madam, which I think should be satisfactory to all parties."

"What's that?"

"Buy the house, madam, take it down stone by stone and ship it to California."

"And put it up there?" Mrs. Spottsworth beamed. "Why, what a brilliant idea!"

"Thank you, madam."

"William Randolph Hearst used to do it, didn't he? I remember visiting at San Simeon once, and there was a whole French Abbey lying on the grass near the gates. I'll do it, Jeeves. You've solved everything. Oh, Lord Rowcester," said Mrs. Spottsworth. "Just the man I wanted to see."

Bill had come in with Jill, walking with slow, despondent steps. As he saw the pendant, despondency fell from him like a garment. Unable to speak, he stood pointing a trembling finger.

"It was discovered in the grass adjoining a rustic seat in the garden, m'lord, by Mrs. Spottsworth's fiancé, Captain Biggar," said Jeeves.

Bill found speech, though with difficulty.

"Biggar's back?"

"Yes, m'lord."

"And he found the pendant?"

"Yes, m'lord."

"And he's engaged to Mrs. Spottsworth?"

"Yes, m'lord. And Mrs. Spottsworth has decided to purchase the Abbey."

"What!"

"Yes, m'lord."

"I do believe in fairies!" said Bill, and Jill said she did, too.

"Yes, Billiken," said Mrs. Spottsworth. "I'm going to buy the Abbey. I don't care what you're asking for it. I want it, and I'll write you a cheque the moment I come back from apologizing to that nice Chief Constable. I left him very abruptly just now, and I'm afraid he may be feeling offended. Is he still up in my room, Jeeves?"

"I believe so, madam. He rang for me not long ago to ask if I could provide him with a magnifying glass."

"I'll go and see him," said Mrs. Spottsworth. "I'm taking the Abbey with me to America, Billiken. It was Jeeves's idea."

She went out, and Jill hurled herself into Bill's arms.

"Oh, Bill! Oh, Bill! Oh, Bill!" she cried. "Though I don't know why I'm kissing you," she said. "I ought to be kissing Jeeves. Shall I kiss you, Jeeves?"

"No, miss."

"Just think, Jeeves. You'll have to buy that fish slice after all."

"It will be a pleasure and a privilege, miss."

"Of course, Jeeves," said Bill, "you must never leave us, wherever we go, whatever we do."

Jeeves sighed apologetically.

"I am very sorry, m'lord, but I fear I cannot avail myself of your kindness. Indeed, I fear I am compelled to hand in my notice."

"Oh, Jeeves!"

"With the deepest regret, miss, I need scarcely say. But Mr. Wooster needs me. I received a letter from him this morning."

"Has he left that school of his, then?"

Jeeves sighed again. "Expelled, m'lord."

"Good heavens!"

"It is all most unfortunate, m'lord. Mr. Wooster was awarded the prize for sock-darning. Two pairs of his socks were actually exhibited on Speech Day. It was then discovered that he had used a crib . . . an old woman whom he smuggled into his study at night."

"Poor old Bertie!"

"Yes, m'lord. I gather from the tone of his communication that the scandal has affected him deeply. I feel that my place is at his side."

Rory came in from the library, looking moody.

"I can't fix it," he said.

"Rory," said Bill, "do you know what's happened?"

"Yes, old boy, I've bust the television set."

"Mrs. Spottsworth is going to marry Captain Biggar, and she's buying the Abbey."

"Oh?" said Rory. His manner was listless. "Well, as I was saying, I can't fix the bally thing, and I don't believe any of the local yokels can, either, so the only thing to do is to go to the fountain head." He went to the telephone. "Give me Square one two three four," he said.

Captain Biggar came bustling through the French window, humming a Swahili wedding march.

"Where's my Rosie?" he asked.

"Upstairs," said Bill. "She'll be down in a minute. She's just been telling us the news. Congratulations, Captain."

"Thank you, thank you."

"I say," said Rory, the receiver at his ear, "I've just remembered another one. Which is bigger, Captain Biggar or Mrs. Biggar? Mrs. Biggar, because she became Biggar. Ha, ha. Ha, ha, ha! Meanwhile, I'm trying to get——"

His number came through.

"Oh, hullo," he said. "Harrige's?"